AMERICA: NO PURCHASE NECESSARY

A Novel

Randolph Randy Camp

Copyright © 2021 Randolph Randy Camp
All rights reserved.

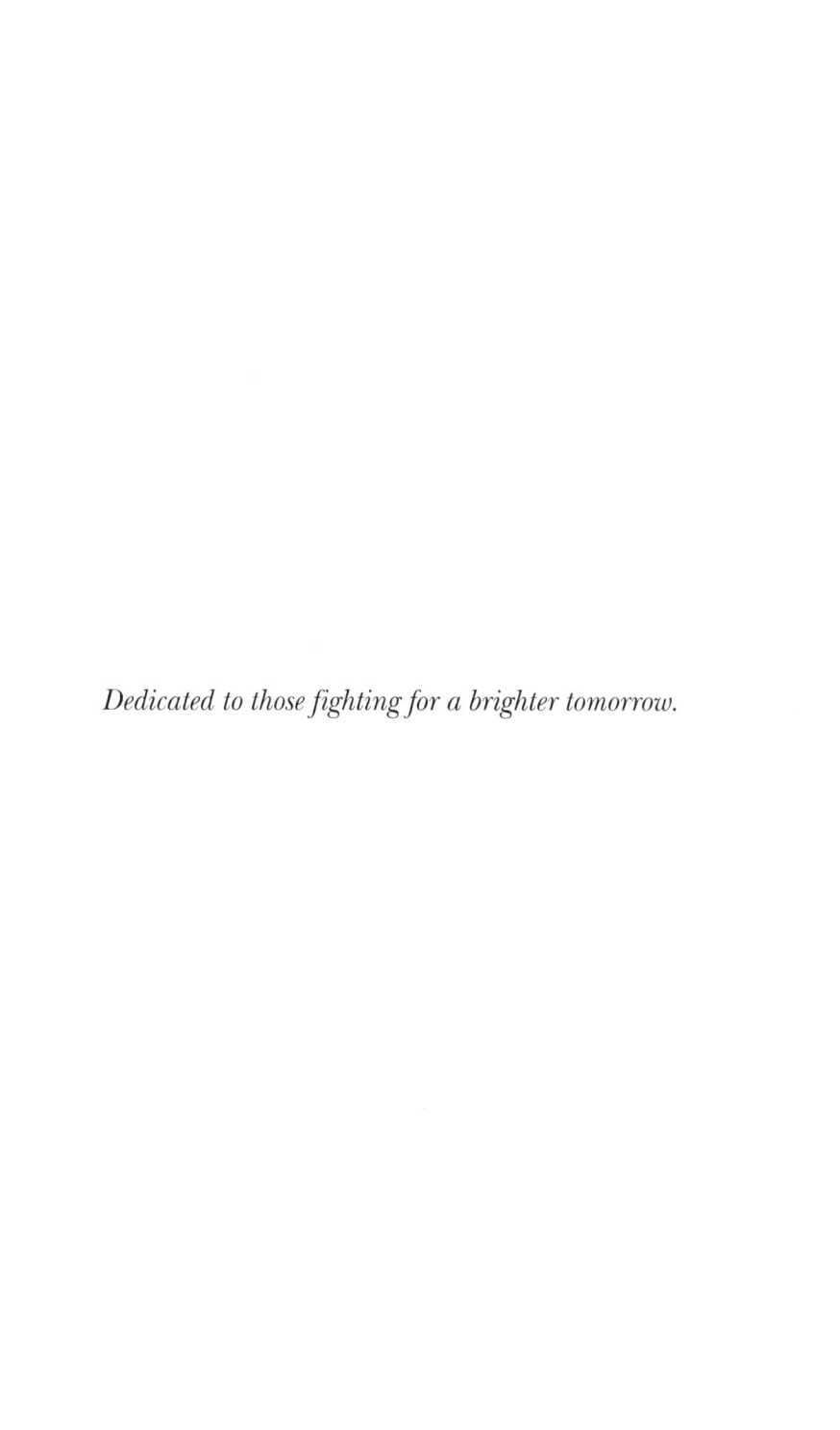

Dedicated to those fighting for a brighter tomorrow.

CHAPTER LIST

Chapter 1	Color This World	1
Chapter 2	You're A Winner	16
Chapter 3	America's Family	21
Chapter 4	Misty's World	25
Chapter 5	Terri's Dream	32
Chapter 6	Splendid Beauty	46
Chapter 7	Brittany's Way	65
Chapter 8	The Gift	95
Chapter 9	April Rising	132
Chapter 10	Latoya's Dilemma	136
Chapter 11	Hollywood	140
Chapter 12	Sunflowers	165
Chapter 13	Tomorrow	175
Epilogue		179
About The Author		183

CHAPTER 1
COLOR THIS WORLD

I'm wearing my good jeans today. These 'the ones that only got one stain on it. But Miss Pritchett says if you tell a good enough story up there then ain't nobody gonna be lookin' at your holes or the stains anyway. I really like Miss Pritchett. She's the best teacher I ever had here at Camden Middle. When Big Riley was making fun of me one day 'cause I was reading a book on the playground instead of playing with the other kids Miss Pritchett came over right away and made him stop. And then she did something that kind of surprised everybody.

Miss Pritchett told Big Riley that his punishment was to get up in front of the whole class the next day and tell everybody why he likes to pick on other kids.

The next day when Riley got up in front of the class, he looked really nervous and didn't know what to say at first. And then Big Riley asked Miss Pritchett if he could sit in a chair, instead of standing. Big Riley got a big ol' round stomach and we all could see his legs shaking a little bit so the teacher let him grab a chair from beside her desk.

Finally, Big Riley started talking and the whole classroom got really quiet. That was the first time I'd ever heard our class get that quiet. The thoughts in Riley's head must've been pretty bad 'cause his tears came way before any words out of his mouth. We'd never seen Big Riley like that before.

"My stepfather never liked me. He likes my mom and my sister though. When he had his friends over to watch a game or some'em he'd called me 'twinkie boy' in front of 'em and then they all would laugh at me. I 'get so mad inside I wanted to beat them up but I knew I couldn't so I guess that's why I pick on little kids instead", Riley breaks as tears continually streak down his cheeks.

Ever since that day Big Riley never picked on me or anybody else ever again. The school nurse had recommended this clinic in town for Riley, to help him lose weight, and it's the same clinic I go to for my autism. Sometimes I see Riley there and we talk. We ain't like best friends now or anything like that but we talk about stuff though.

Miss Pritchett started her first 'Sit n' Talk' with Big Riley but now we have it once a month. Miss Pritchett lets us sit in the chair, just like Riley did, in front of everybody and we get to say whatever we wanna say. We can tell stories, made up ones or real-life ones too. She even let us cuss if we want to, but she says if we do use cuss words it better be part of the story. Miss Pritchett says the principal would shut the whole 'Sit n' Talk' thing down if we started cussing just to be funny or some'em.

Right now Monica Mennison is up there telling her story. Some of the kids in the class said that they don't like Monica's stories 'cause they're always about death and people dying. Last year when me and Monica was in the fifth grade together she'd told me how she and her mom had found her father dead on the floor from doing too much crystal. At first I didn't know what crystal was but now I know a whole lot about meth, heroine, and other drugs too 'cause of what Monica be telling me.

We've been doing the 'Sit n' Talk' thing for awhile now. Everybody likes it. They're so cool 'cause we can sit and talk twenty minutes or we can stay up there for two hours if we wanted to. It don't matter. Our teacher says that expressing yourself and telling your story is what's important. The time it takes to tell it don't really matter she says.

I swear, Miss Pritchett is the coolest. She just sits in the back of the class just like she's one of us. I never seen her interrupt us when we're up there talking either. She just lets us do our thing and the only time she says anything is when the story is finished and then she'll asked the class if we have any questions.

At our last 'Sit n' Talk' last month Monica talked about how everybody was going to die 'cause of global warming and climate change and how people, especially the grownups in charge, wasn't doing enough to stop it. Today, Monica's telling us about kids taking over the government and creating their own state for themselves. Most of the time I tell made-up stories but today I'm telling my first real life story.

I'm glad I'm wearing my good pants 'cause I'm real excited today. It's my turn right after Monica finishes her talk. Sometimes I can tell when somebody's about to end their story 'cause you can tell by their facial expressions sometimes and how fast or slow their words come out, but with Monica though, it's just too hard to tell 'cause her face don't really change all that much. She always kind of got that same ol' face that looks kind of mean and serious all 'the time like she might hurt you or some'em.

"Some kids' IQ level is way higher than some of these adult politicians we got right now so that's why voting should be based on a person's IQ level and not their age," Monica abruptly finishes.

"Do anyone have any questions for Monica?", Miss Pritchett promptly asks.

In the second row, Troy raises his hand.

"Go ahead, Troy", Miss Pritchett nods.

"In your story Monica you said that the adults may have to leave if the kids start their own state. How will the kids get the adults to leave if the adults don't wanna leave?", Troy asks with a puzzled face.

Deadly serious, Monica wastes no time firing back with her no-nonsense response, "Like I said in the beginning, all adults will be eliminated if they don't comply."

We've been scared by Monica's stories before but this one today is making everybody feel a different kind of scared. Monica looks straight at Troy, sort of checking to see if she'd answered his question. Troy ain't saying a word. Ain't nobody saying nothing. Then Miss Pritchett breaks the ice, "If there's no more questions for Monica then Ronnie you're up," she says with a slight sigh of relief.

When we first started we were using that ol' hard wooden chair beside Miss Pritchett's desk but now we got a better one with a soft cushion on it. I like that 'cause my stories usually be pretty long. And on the blackboard behind us Miss Pritchett always write 'Sit n' Talk Day!' in big fat letters.

Everybody's eyes are glued on Ronnie as he's about to start his story. Just about everybody enjoys Ronnie's stories because they're very detailed. Ronnie's doctor at the clinic he goes to says that his autism isn't always a bad thing because sometimes there are some benefits too, like when Ronnie be seeing and explaining the tiniest things that other people may take for granted or possibly they didn't even realize it was there in the first place.

"The story I'm going to tell y'all today don't really have a title or anything 'cause it's kind of just about my family. Y'all might've heard some things about my family from that big contest we won but today I'm gonna tell y'all the real deal about that contest and all the stuff that went down last year," Ronnie coolly nods.

It all started last summer on Ferry Avenue when the Camden Devils was just chilling and listening to some jams under the only shade tree on Ferry. It's a big dogwood tree right in front of Mister Red Coles' yard. The Camden Devils always tells cops that they ain't a real gang, that they're just friends hanging out. But people on my street knows that ain't true 'cause last spring they raped a girl in one of 'em abandoned houses on Linwood. Everybody knows 'they did it but ain't nobody talking though. Even the girls in the Devils don't even say nothing about it.

All of the Devils always be wearing something with the color orange on it, an orange shirt, an orange blouse, orange shorts, orange sneakers, or orange bandanas. They never wear red or blue 'cause those are already taken. Some people don't like the Devils hanging around but they don't bother me. One day they started calling me 'Books' because they would always see me carrying books or coming from the library. If people don't bother them then they don't bother nobody. But some people though, like ol' man Red Coles just don't like the Devils at all.

Mister Coles is the only White man living on Ferry. His house is only two houses over from ours. Mister Coles lives alone but he got a grownup daughter that for some reason won't come to visit him. People around here just calls him Red. Mister Coles is the same age as my Grandma Fannie and they both came from the South too. They both got 'em old-fashioned Southern ways that people here in Jersey sometimes don't understand. And to be honest with you me and my grandma are kind of close but there's still some things about her I don't know. Grandma Fannie tells me a lot of stuff but there's parts of her she keeps to herself. Grandma says 'my ears are too small for some things. I don't even know if it's true or not but years ago, before I was born, people said that there was a block party in the neighborhood and my Grandma Fannie and Mister Coles got so drunk 'they'd ended up in Mister Coles' bed together the next morning. People said it's true but my grandma ain't never said nothing about it to me though. Deep down I kind of think it's true 'cause whenever I see them too standing close to each other they both act kind of funny, like they know some'em that ain't nobody else be knowing. To me, I think that the only thing keeping my Grandma Fannie and ol' man Red Coles apart is their skin color. Everybody got a past but the kind of past my grandma and Red got ain't the kind they like to talk about.

The Jersey sun ain't playing around today so there's a bunch of 'em Devils chilling in the shade under that big dogwood. Rap music is blaring from two mini-speakers connected to somebody's cellphone leaning against the trunk of the dogwood. I'd just checked out two books from the library and I was on my way home when I saw Mister Coles running out of his house with the meanest look on his face! Red was headed straight towards the Devils just a few feet from his front yard.

"Y'all need to get the hell out of my yard with that loud ass noise!", Mister Coles angrily barks.

Defiantly, one of the Devils springs up to face Mister Coles, "First of all old man, we ain't in yo' yard n' you need to check yo'self n' come at us with some respect."

"Respect? How 'bout y'all respecting me and this whole neighborhood by turning off that loud stupid noise you people call rap!", Mister Coles fires back and then adds, "I got a shotgun and it's ready to go!"

Anybody on Ferry could hear them arguing. Hard words were flying back and forth! As I was coming down the sidewalk and getting closer one of the Devils turned to me, "Yo' Books, you better go get yo' Grandmother to cool this fool down before we do some'em crazy 'round here."

The Devil was right. If anybody could calm Mister Coles down it would only be my Grandma Fannie. She just got this certain way with people. Maybe it's a Southern thing. I don't know. But Grandma would always tell me that most 'times if there's some food or good music around while you're talking and discussing things then a lot of problems would get solved. But she says if food or music ain't helping none then you know something must be really wrong. Grandma says that when you're in the thick mud, the kind of mud that pulls your shoes off.

Hurriedly, Ronnie dashes down the street to his house. He tosses his two library books on the couch then quickly finds his Grandma Fannie in the kitchen.

"Grandma! Grandma! They need you! Mister Coles says he's going to get his shotgun 'cause the

Devils 'playing their music too loud!", Ronnie anxiously warns.

"Oh Lord, here we go again," Grandma Fannie sighs then quickly adds, "Baby, go in my bedroom, look in the third drawer in my big dresser and get my Linda Martell 'Color Me Country' CD. I'll meet you at Red's place."

When Grandma Fannie was a little girl growing up in South Carolina her mother taught her how to cook and season foods with what was available from the land around them 'cause Black people were too poor to buy meats and other kind of stuff from the store back then. So they used beans a lot as the main part of the meal back then. Grandma Fannie got these special recipes for the way she seasons her butter beans and navy beans. People come from miles away asking for my grandma's seasoned beans.

Grandma Fannie was in the midst of boiling a pot of beans when Ronnie popped in. She turns off the flames under the steaming pot, opens the refrigerator and retrieves a bowl-size, leftover container filled with some of her best seasoned butter beans then rush out the house!

Things are boiling over under the big dogwood as Grandma Fannie arrives just in time to break up the shouting match between Mister Coles and the Devils.

Grandma Fannie shoots Mister Coles a scornful eye then skillfully speaks with a soft tone, "Red, I don't think anybody out here is causing any trouble. It's hot as hell and they just needed some shade."

"Yeah n' this ol' fool came out here calling us 'you people' like he's somebody n' better than us or some'em," one of the Devils interjects.

Grandma Fannie gives Mister Coles another scornful look.

"Look Fannie, they come around here and start playing that damn crap they call music so loud it's just plain irritating and rude!", Mister Coles pleads, then adds, "maybe if they played some real music instead of that rap crap that you can't even understand because half the time it's not even real words they're saying. Who wants to listen to that mumbling crap at full blast?"

People always say that you can tell a lot about a person from the music they listen to and when I opened my grandma's third drawer of her big dresser I was blown away when I saw all of those colorful CD's. The drawer was filled with country singers, rock n' roll bands, soul singers, and even some Cajun zydeco bands too. Her music drawer looked like a rainbow. Even though people didn't always like her just because of her skin color I always knew my grandma loved everybody though, and her music drawer proved it. I kept shifting the CD's around for a few minutes and then I finally spotted the CD I was looking for. With that bright colored CD in my hand I took off out of the room.

"So what you're saying ol' man is that if we was playing that hillbilly stuff then you'd be okay with that?", one of the Devils taunts.

"All I'm saying is that Willie and Waylon played music, real music. I don't know what the hell rap is but it sure ain't music," Mister Coles provokes.

In the nick of time, Ronnie flies down the sidewalk with the CD then hands it to his grandmother as she coolly, in her smooth unique way, strategically steps in between Mister Coles and the tensed-up Devils.

Smartly using her Southern charm and delicate tone, Grandma Fannie turns to the Devils, "Listen y'all, is it any way y'all can turn the volume down a little bit when y'all come around here?"

Not waiting for an answer from the Devils, Grandma Fannie quickly turns to Mister Coles, handing him the plastic container of her seasoned butter beans and the CD Ronnie had just brought over, "Red, when you and me were about ten years old in '69 a big country hit song was playing on the radio all that summer and it's on that CD in your hand right there."

America: No Purchase Necessary

Mister Coles' eyes nearly popped out of his head when he looked at the smiling face of the Black lady on the CD cover, "A colored girl singing country?"

A few of the Devils begin to giggle, "Did he just say 'colored girl'?", one of them quips.

"Red, that's Linda Martell. Everybody played her song 'Color Him Father' that summer. I know you still got that old CD player I gave you two Christmas' ago so go ahead and take a listen to it while you're eating that fresh bowl of seasoned beans I made this morning," Grandma Fannie says with a suggestive nod.

As my Grandma Fannie was cooling things down on Ferry, my brother Terri and his friend Jay are hanging out at Family Time Burgers down on Westchester a few blocks away. My brother is always broke but he always watches for the free French fries coupon that Family Time Burgers sends out in the mail every now and then. My brother's real name is Terrance but he and most of his closest friends feel like a girl inside so he likes it better when people call him Terri. I don't understand all of my brother's stuff, like when he and his friends dress like girls, but in a weird kind of way I understand him a little bit 'cause it's kind of like when sometimes I don't feel like doing stuff other kids my age be doing 'cause sometimes I don't feel eleven. A lot of times I feel like I'm about twenty-two inside. My brother Terri finished high school last year but now he's kind of in limbo 'cause his grades weren't that great to get him into college but I know he wants to do something better with his life instead of just hanging around Camden and doing nothing. He likes legal stuff. One time there was this TV marathon of that old lawyer TV show 'Boston Legal' and Terri didn't miss one episode.

Terri and his friends kind of stick close together 'cause some people don't treat them right. When Terri goes to Family Time Burgers he only goes when his favorite waitress is working. She's been working there for fifteen years and she's kind of like my Grandma Fannie. She loves everybody, no matter what. When Terri goes to Family Time Burgers and if he doesn't see Charlene working then he'll turn around and go back home.

The Family Time Burgers down on Westchester Street is always busy. It's one of the nicer-looking places in that area. Terri and Jay are sitting at a booth along the windows looking out at one of Camden's struggling neighborhoods. Terri's bleach blonde hair, earrings and lipstick makes people stare but he'd told me that he just ignores them. While waiting for Charlene to over, Terri and Jay are discussing the current developments with the proper pronoun situation.

"So, I just spent all this time getting people to call me Terri, instead of Terrance, and now I have to school them again on how to use 'they' when they're talking about me?", Terri sighs.

"Terri, it's hard being trans these days. We gotta be school teachers now," Jay quips with a smile.

Cheerfully, Charlene arrives at the booth, "Hey, hey, what's it gonna be today?"

Right away, Terri and Jay each hands Charlene their coupon for a free order of fries.

"And hey, before I forget, why don't y'all enter our big sweepstakes while you're waiting," Charlene suggests as she happily slides the colorful sheets atop the table along with two ink pens.

"But don't you have to spend like ten or twenty dollars or some'em here first though?", Jay asks.

"Nope. No purchase necessary. Just answer a few questions about our service and that's it", Charlene quickly replies.

Terri scans the few questions on the colorful survey sheet then gladly starts to fill it out.

CHAPTER 2
YOU'RE A WINNER

It's three weeks later and something extraordinary is about to happen on Ferry Avenue today. The glistening afternoon sun illuminates a vibrant red, white, and blue full-size luxury RV as it slowly cruises down the street flanked with rundown homes and abandoned lots. 'FAMILY TIME CORPORATION'S AMERICA'S FAMILY SWEEPSTAKES' is painted in bold letters along the side of the deluxe RV. The colorful mobile home crawls to a stop curbside at 312 Ferry Avenue, where a weathered bungalow is fronted with a broken gate. This is the home of the Lanterns, Ronnie's family.

With flowers, balloons, and an oversized $50,000 check in hand, Sherry Will and two of her sweepstakes staffers step out of the shiny RV then cheerfully head towards the front steps. Holding the string of colorful balloons, Sherry knocks on the front door.

My mother, Darcy Lantern, answers the door with that cautious look of hers. My mom always tell people 'she's twenty-eight but she's forty for real. For the last five years she's been twenty-eight though. Looking at the bountiful flowers and vibrant balloons, my mother asks, "What's this?"

"Hi, my name is Sherry Will from the Family Time Corporation. Is there a Terrance Lantern residing here?"

"I'm telling y'all right now, I ain't the one y'all need to be messing with today. I got no problem beating yo' skinny ass in front of yo' two friends here if this is some kind of bullshit prank."

⊷⊶

"I assure you this is not a prank. Terrance Lantern is the winner of our nationwide America's Family Sweepstakes."

My mom still ain't convinced yet. My mother's been living in Camden so long that she thinks everybody's got a hustle and some people ain't to be trusted no matter what especially if they're always hanging in the streets. My mom shoots Sherry that cautious eye again, "But how could my son win anything when he ain't never got no money? He can't afford to buy no tickets, no raffles, no lotto, no scratch offs, no nothing. He ain't never got no money."

Sherry smiles at Darcy's skepticism then says with a reassuring nod, "Ma'am, he won fair and square. Just like millions of others across America he simply filled out a survey with no purchase necessary. He won that RV parked by your curb right there. He gets fifty grand cash, gets a meet and greet with the President of the United States, plus a fully paid cross-country road trip with stops at our Family Time Restaurants where the whole entire family will participate in three live TV commercials! Is Terrance here? Can we meet him?"

I think Sherry just convinced my mom that this is totally legit. My mom is speechless.

"America's Family? Hm," Darcy shakes her head in disbelief.

Awestruck, Darcy steps inside and yells for her oldest son, "Terri!"

Seconds later, Sherry and her two sweepstakes staffers are taken aback when a flamboyant Terri appears at the door with a feminine swag, short blonde hair and fresh lipstick.

Terri's face gleams while eyeing the roomy RV, oversized check, bountiful flowers and colorful balloons.

"For real? For me?", Terri questions with a feminine tone.

"If you're Terrance Lantern then you're our winner," Sherry nods reassuringly.

The vibrant acrylic nails of Terri's hand momentarily distract Sherry's attention as the lively eighteen-year-old offers a handshake, "Hi, you can call me Terri."

Unbeknownst to Sherry and Terri standing at the doorway, Darcy was already inside the house going room to room, excitedly telling the rest of the family about Terri winning the sweepstakes, "Y'all guess what? We're going on a vacation! That no-job, broke-ass Terri done went and won a big ol' contest! We fixin' to go on a road trip in one of 'em real fancy houses-on-wheels-looking things! We're getting the hell out of Camden! Y'all hurry up and pack yo' stuff before they change their minds!"

Sherry can't seem to take her eyes off of Terri's earrings and bleach blonde hair as she shakes his hand at the doorway. Then, abruptly, to their surprise, they are both brushed aside by the rest of the Lantern family as they hurriedly burst through the front door, one by one, with each carrying a packed suitcase!

First out the door is Terri's mother Darcy, then Terri's father Reggie swiftly flies out the door followed by Terri's hot looking sixteen-year-old sister Latoya and her heavily-tattooed, sixteen-year-old Mexican boyfriend Rico Garcia, along with Terri's book nerd, younger brother Ronnie and their sweet, straightforward Southern-born Grandma Fannie trailing behind.

The entire Lantern clan spill out unto the front lawn, each placing their luggage on the ground then simultaneously, they all shoot Terri and the sweepstakes staff a look that says 'We're ready! Let's go!'

Somewhat amused and perplexed at the same time, Sherry and her two sweepstakes staffers inconspicuously glance at one another with uneasy smiles, trying their best to conceal the fact that they truly did not expect a Black family to be the winner of their nationwide sweepstakes.

Sherry, wearing that big put-on grin of hers, eyes the eager family members then unleashes the string of colorful balloons into the air!

"Congratulations everyone! You're America's Family!", Sherry cheers.

CHAPTER 3
AMERICA'S FAMILY

Meanwhile, in the stately office of Jake Astor, the CEO of the Family Time Corporation Headquarters, nestled in Fairfax, Virginia, proud American patriotism screams blatantly loud and clear. Elegant, framed paintings of various Family Time Restaurants and Family Time RV Dealerships across the nation highlight the walls as the company's trademarked vibrant red, white and blue roofs and awnings certainly grabs the attention.

Ornamenting the wall above the CEO's enormous, glossy oak desk is a poster-size framed selfie photo of the current U.S. President Dennis Wheeler and Jake Astor holding golf clubs on a prestigious golf green.

In the left corner of the office, on the plush green carpet, Jake is intensely studying the angle of his next shot as he softly swings his golf club over a golf ball a few feet from an overturned trash can.

In between meetings with his staff, Jake never passes up an opportunity to practice his golf shots. In a few minutes Jake is having a scheduled meeting with Sherry Will.

There's a soft knock at the door. "Com'on in, Sherry," Jake answers.

Looking a bit apprehensive, Sherry walks in carrying a vanilla folder. Jake leans his golf club against the wall then takes a seat at his desk.

"So, how'd it go, Sherry? Tell me about this Terrance Lantern and our new America's Family. I bet they were excited about the meet and greet with President Wheeler, huh?," Jake excitedly asks.

Sherry doesn't offer a direct response to Jake's question. Instead, Sherry takes enlarged photos of Terri and the Lantern family out of the vanilla folder then places them atop Jake's desk.

Jake sighs and deflates in disappointment while scanning the various photos of black and brown faces.

"This is America's Family?", Jakes asks with a twisted frown.

Half-heartedly, Sherry nods yes. Reluctantly, Jake takes a closer look at the pictures. Jake can't hide his emotions as he cringes in disgust while eyeing the numerous tattoos on Rico.

"Who is that? Looks like he's a member of one of them street gangs. And what's that on his neck?", Jake asks while shaking his head.

Sherry leans in for a closer look at the photo.

Nonchalantly, Sherry replies, "Oh that's Rico. He's the boyfriend of the winner's sister Latoya, and I believe that's a snake on his neck. No, no, wait, my mistake. I think that's a dragon."

Jakes sighs then continually shakes his head in disbelief.

Jake begins to shuffle and scatter the enlarged photos atop his desk. "So, which one is our winner Terrance Lantern?", Jake turns to Sherry with a curious eye.

Sherry points to a photo of Terri that accentuates his trimmed eye brows and luscious eyelashes.

Baffled, Jake gives Sherry a look.

Ensuring that her boss gets the point that Terri is definitely not your typical guy, Sherry points out another photo of Terri which accentuates his dangling earrings and bleach blonde hair.

"He likes to be called Terri. I think he's trans," Sherry elaborates.

"Trans? The winner of our nationwide sweepstakes is a transexual? We have to disqualify him, her, whatever. We have a problem here, Sherry, a big problem. Can we get another family?"

"Can't. Legally can't. Terri filled out and submitted the survey just like everybody else. And, I think the proper term is transgender, not transexual."

"We're up shit's creek, Sherry. President Wheeler ain't gonna like this one bit."

CHAPTER 4
MISTY'S WORLD

It's another typical busy day in Washington, DC, where the President of the United States tries his best to inform the American people about his current agenda. But some reporters are smart enough to know that not everything that goes on in Washington is on the up and up.

The White House press room is jammed with TV camera crews, reporters, journalists and photographers. White House Press Secretary Misty Madsen is alone at the podium fielding questions from reporters.

New York World reporter Brittany Stills raise her hand and is quickly given a nod by Misty at the podium.

"What is the White House response to violation allegations pertaining to the President's reelection campaign fund, specifically relating to large financial contributions from Jake Astor and his Family Time Corporation?", Brittany asks.

Somewhat evasively, Misty tries to dodge Brittany's question, "Look, we'd called this press conference today because the President just signed the new immigration bill to protect our borders. Maybe some of your other concerns can be addressed at another time. Next question, please."

Brittany is startled by Misty's cold response, "Are you just going to blow me off like that, Misty? The public has the right to know these things."

Scanning the room, Misty seemingly mouths 'Bitch' while totally avoiding any direct eye contact with Brittany Stills. Other reporters hastily raise their hands. Misty points to a reporter seated in the rear corner.

Brittany refuses to be ignored. She boldly interjects, "Really, Misty? Did you just call me a bitch?"

Again, Misty ignores Brittany's question as she nods to the reporter in the back, "Yes, the gentleman in the corner, please."

Showing a sense of solidarity among reporters, the gentleman in the rear corner basically reiterates Brittany's original question, "Is President Wheeler's reelection campaign or the President himself being paid big money to meet with the winning family of the Family Time Corporation national sweepstakes, and is the House Ethics Committee aware of these large financial contributions?"

Abruptly, Misty hastily gathers her notepad from the podium while avoiding any eye contact with the reporter in the rear corner.

"Sorry, folks. We're out of time," Misty announces with a frosty smile.

Everyone in the press room is baffled as Misty leaves the podium then disappears through a side door.

A short distance away, in the Oval Office, U.S. President Dennis Wheeler, along with his shifty-eye, reelection campaign manager Nick Bennet, and key members of the President's staff, are enjoying carry-out orders of burgers and fries while standing in front of a bank of five wide-screen TV monitors along the left wall.

Several trademarked red, white and blue carry-out bags from Family Time Burgers are scattered atop the office furniture. Each of the five TV screens, from national broadcasters, CBS News, ABC News, CNN News, FOX News, and NBC News, are simultaneously displaying a close-up shot on Misty Madsen's face then zooms in tighter on Misty's lips moving in slow motion, showing her mouthing the word 'bitch' at the press briefing moments ago.

Enthralled by the broadcast on the large screens, everyone in the Oval Office nods approvingly at Misty's unconventional behavior.

One of the staffers turns up the volume on one of the TV monitors, "Folks, we have breaking news. Just moments ago, a reporter from New York World was called a bitch by White House Press Secretary Misty Madsen at today's White House press briefing."

Seconds later, Misty enters the Oval Office and is surprised to see her big wide face on each of the five large TV screens. Immediately, Misty is greeted with congratulatory high-fives from President Dennis Wheeler and his snake-tongue reelection campaign manager Nick Bennett.

"Way to go, Misty! You're right, that Brittany Stills can be a real bitch sometimes," Nick greets with a crooked smirk.

"Great job, Misty. Great job," President Wheeler chimes in.

"Hey guys, just for the record, you know, technically I didn't verbally say bitch. I caught myself and nothing was heard," Misty explains.

Boastfully, Nick points to the wall of widescreen TV monitors where each screen continually shows Misty's lips mouthing the word 'bitch' in slow motion.

"Now that's how you handle the press! Misty, you 'the man! You 'the man!", Nick cheers.

Misty sighs at Nick's celebratory antics then turns to President Wheeler who is digging into the bottom of a Family Time Burgers carry-out bag, trying to retrieve a few scattered fries at the bottom.

"Mister President, I know that Jake Astor is your golfing buddy and one of your closest friends, but I really need to know if you're making any kind of financial deals with Jake or his Family Time Corporation because the press isn't just going to let this one go," Misty pleads.

Avoiding a response, President Wheeler slyly winks at Nick then stuffs a few greasy fries into his mouth.

Nick steps a little closer to Misty, "Hey, Misty, don't worry, we got this all under control. Don't sweat the small stuff. Jake and the President did a simple handshake deal over a golf game and the President is going to do a quick meet and greet, in Saint Louis, in a few weeks with the winning family of that big national sweepstakes contest Jake's running. Misty, we got this. Don't worry. It's all under control. You just handle the press. We got the rest."

Misty sighs at Nick's conniving ways, while President Wheeler digs into another red, white and blue carry-out bag then tosses Misty a Family Time burger.

"They're really good," President Wheeler nods.

Unenthused, Misty catches the wrapped burger then sighs in frustration.

I don't think 'Misty started out bad but probably ever since she started working with them snakes in the White House then that's when she probably got bad too. My Grandma Fannie says 'there's a lot of snakes in places you don't expect to see 'em. Misty probably didn't know when to get out, that's all. Grandma Fannie used an outside bathroom when she was little in South Carolina and she would always tell me that if you stayed in the outhouse too long you might come out smelling like poop so it's best to just do whatever you gotta do n' get the hell out of there the fast as you can. I think maybe Misty probably done stayed in the outhouse too long.

Some kids my age don't care about stuff in Washington 'cause they say that they can't do anything about it. But Miss Pritchett told us that we should always keep up on our current events 'cause we should always know what's going on around us. I like knowing what's going on and I like reading the articles in New York World, especially those ones that Brittany Stills writes. Brittany Stills is real good n' she won big time news awards too! She don't beat around the bush either. Brittany tells it like it is, for real. Sometimes, people still be making fun of me 'cause I like to read grownup news magazines but I don't care though 'cause at least I know what's happening in the

America: No Purchase Necessary

world. And that's another reason why I like reading Brittany Stills' stuff too 'cause she always says that not everybody in Washington cares about the world. Brittany says that a lot of people in Washington getting those big fat paychecks and wearing those new suits sometimes only care about themselves n' not the people who voted for them. Brittany Stills don't care if you're the President of the United States or a regular street person, she'll tell the world about you, especially if you're doing something dirty.

⇌

CHAPTER 5
TERRI'S DREAM

We're on the road now. This is so exciting! I've never been anywhere outside of Camden. Whenever I'm reading a book that takes place outside of New Jersey I always wish and hope that one day I get a chance to go there in person one day. This cross-country trip we're taking now is gonna make that dream come true.

This big fancy RV we're traveling in sure is catching everybody's attention. When we're on the highway people turn their heads at us, and every place we stop for gas people just stare at us. I think people can't help but look at us 'cause we look like a big ol' flag. That big company that owns all of 'em Family Time Burgers and RV dealerships got everything of theirs painted red, white and blue. I guess they really want people to know that they're American, I guess.

America: No Purchase Necessary

Right now we're on Interstate 70 going west towards Dayton, Ohio. My father Reggie is behind the wheel. My father likes driving. He was in the Army years ago where he used to work on jeeps and trucks, and when he wasn't fixing things he said that he used to drive the officers around the base. I think my father called his unit 'motor pool' or some'em like that. Back in Camden my father works part-time at a factory but I know he don't like it there though 'cause all he ever talks about is having his own tour bus business one day.

My mom Darcy is sitting up front in the passenger seat. She's just looking around and enjoying the scenery as we cruise along in heavy traffic.

⊷⊶

This big fancy RV thing gotta big ol' living room area just behind the driver and passenger seat, and that's where me and my brother Terri is comfortably sitting. I like to help out whenever I can so I'm studying an old fold-out road map plus I'm double-checking the directions with the GPS on my mom's cellphone too. My brother Terri has a small makeup mirror propped up on the coffee table as he carefully applies fresh eyeliner around his eyes.

"Dad, we're getting close to the Dayton exit. It should be coming up soon on the right," Ronnie alerts his father.

Reggie looks over towards the passenger side mirror, steps on the gas then swiftly maneuvers the enormous mobile home into the far-right lane as Terri's eyeliner brush slightly slips from his fingers, creating a black streak across his right cheek.

"Ughhh! See Mama, I told you not to let Dad drive. He 'be having a little too much fun sitting behind that wheel. He's probably drunk," Terri teases.

Playfully, Reggie replies, "I ain't drunk. I'm just having a good ol' time driving this big sexy thang. Hm, I ain't drove something this big n' sexy since me and your mother used to ----".

"Big? Whatcha mean 'big'?", Darcy interrupts while giving her husband the eye.

Smartly, Reggie changes the subject.

"Terri, why 'you're putting that stuff on now anyway?", Reggie asks while glancing at Terri's makeup fiasco in the rear-view mirror.

Terri snatches a napkin from a tissue box atop the coffee table then wipes the streak from his cheek.

"Remember what Sherry said? We got our first live TV commercial in Dayton and I don't know about y'all but Terri Lantern is gonna be ready," Terri nods with confidence.

Ronnie spots the Dayton exit ramp a short distance ahead.

"That's our exit coming up, Dad", Ronnie excitedly points.

A short time later, Ronnie and the entire Lantern family enters Family Time Burgers where they will be shooting the first of three live TV commercials as 'America's Family'. Sherry and another colleague from the corporate office of Family Time headquarters greets the Lanterns near the entrance area.

The same patriotic color scheme and atmosphere as Jake Astor's office, the interior decor of this bustling Family Time Burgers loudly yells American pride with its red, white and blue tabletops, framed paintings of the American flag, Mount Rushmore, and the Washington Monument ornamenting the walls.

There's a mix of excitement and organized chaos in the spacious diner as a TV camera crew sets up lighting and sound equipment around a lengthy table while hordes of hungry customers glance around at the busy TV crew with curious eyes.

Feeling apprehensive about an African-American family being the face of his massive Family Time Corporation, CEO Jake Astor had asked Sherry to meet up with the Lantern family periodically along their cross-country trip to ensure that things go as smoothly as possible.

Sherry is standing near the entrance huddled with Terri and the other six members of the Lantern family. Standing alongside Sherry is Meghan Whitman, the perky, blonde spokesperson for Family Time Restaurants. At age forty-three, Meghan looks gorgeous and is always camera-ready. Meghan's young hair stylist is brushing Meghan's long, seductive hair while trying her best not to be in the way.

Sherry gets a nod from the camera director, signaling that they are almost ready to shoot.

Sherry starts her briefing with the Lanterns, "Everybody, if you hadn't already noticed, this is Meghan standing next to me. I'm sure you've seen her on TV in quite a few of our commercials for Family Time Burgers. When I get the cue for you to take your seats Meghan will come around the table and ask you a few simple questions. Remember, there's no script so say whatever comes to mind. We're shooting this live because we want to capture the essence of an honest, authentic American family. The kitchen already got everybody's orders so the wait staff should be bringing out your food any time now. Is everybody ready?"

With no shortage of confidence and a whole lot of sass, Terri nods to Sherry, "Honey, I'm always ready."

One of the sound engineers from the TV crew gives the director a thumbs up then the director quickly shoots Sherry a nod.

America: No Purchase Necessary

Sherry motions the seven eager family members to take their seats at the table.

⇌⇋

Two cheerful waitresses approach the lengthy table with seven appetizing plates of juicy burgers and bountiful golden fries.

"Hi y'all, welcome to Family Time! We got six classic burgers and one order of our new veggie burger for...Rico?," one of the waitresses politely asks as she scans the table.

Rico quickly raises his hand. Both waitresses are momentarily captivated by Rico's peculiar tattoo of Japanese characters along his right forearm.

"Nice tat," one of the waitresses compliments as she places Rico's veggie burger and fries upon the table.

"Thanks," Rico modestly nods.

Rico is my sister's boyfriend but he and my sister Latoya 'been knowing each other since they were little, little like when they were younger than me. Rico is kind of like a brother to me, almost. Rico's been living with us for a long time now 'cause his parents 'gone. His father got deported back to Mexico and his mom is gone for real. She hung herself one day after two of her friends got deported at the factory she was working at. They made high priced clothes at that factory but they didn't pay the workers right though. Rico don't like to talk about his mom but he started getting all of those tattoos after she killed herself though. Rico's father used to be in the Air Force and he spent a lot of time overseas in Japan. His father used to send him letters and post cards all the time from Japan. Rico would get all excited whenever he got mail from his dad. Rico ain't never went to Japan but I bet 'he could tell you anything you wanted to know about it.

The skeletal TV crew is holding up hovering mikes and lighting shades over the table. Three cameras are getting shots from various angles. One cameraman slowly pans the table, filming and catching brief glimpses of the Lanterns then shifts to Meghan, the perky spokesperson, as she puts on her big TV smile.

"Hey, hey! Today's so special because we're going to meet the Lantern family! Yay! Winners of our Family Time Sweepstakes!", Meghan cheers into the camera.

Seated directly across the table from Rico, Grandma Fannie makes a face then turns up her upper lip while eyeing Rico take a hungry bite of his juicy veggie burger. The rest of the family notices Grandma Fannie's twisted face then nods a knowing smile.

"Okay Mama, just let it out 'cause we know it's coming," Reggie teases with a sigh.

Just as Reggie and the family predicted, Grandma Fannie doesn't waste any time holding back her views on the newfound popularity of certain plant-based foods, "I don't understand all the fuss over these veggie burgers. It's like we're paying somebody to lie to us. What's this world coming to if we wanna be lied to? Nobody likes to be lied to, but yet, we already know it's not real meat. I mean all they're doing is smashing beans n' broccoli together and then shaping it like a round burger. Hell, why do all 'that when you can just order and eat a bowl of beans or some broccoli on the side."

Standing mere inches behind Meghan, Sherry is getting antsy as Grandma Fannie continues her rant. Wearing a nervous grin, Meghan politely refrains from interrupting.

"All I'm saying is why pay somebody to shape it like a round beef burger when we already know that's a lie! Hell, just put a bowl of beans on the menu if people wanna start eating more healthy," Grandma Fannie reiterates.

Meanwhile, in the fourth-floor board room at the Family Time Corporate Headquarters, Jake Astor and his roundtable of executives are watching the Lantern's first live TV appearance on a large, wall-mounted screen. Jake seems genuinely interested in

Grandma Fannie's bowl of beans idea as he rubs his chin, "Hm, I think she might be on to something there. Let's say we put a focus team on this bowl of beans thing and get Sherry to talk to this Grandma Fannie."

Unsurprisingly, every executive nod agreeably.

Back to the live commercial at the Dayton Family Time Burgers, Grandma Fannie looks directly at Rico as he takes another bite out of his veggie burger.

"I betcha it tastes like beans, huh, Rico?," Grandma Fannie says with a twisted smirk.

Sherry immediately pokes Meghan's side, signaling her to quickly intervene before Rico has a chance to respond. Awkwardly, Meghan leans down closer to Rico as he swallows his food. Meghan tries her best to change the subject, "Rico, that's such an interesting tattoo on your arm. So cool how it's written in the traditional characters."

"In Japanese it's 'nana korobi ya oki'. It means 'fall down seven times, get up eight'", Rico nods.

"Hm, I wonder how you say bowl of beans in Japanese," Grandma Fannie interjects with a peculiar look.

The three cameras are panning the Lantern family but neither one is fixated on Terri. Latoya's beautiful face grabs the attention of two cameras! The camera loves her warm, inviting smile. Ever since Latoya was a little girl she'd quietly dreamt of a day like today. Latoya waves and blows air kisses to the cameras as if she's a Hollywood red carpet moment.

Terri glances at Latoya. Terri then looks at the waitress still admiring Rico's tattoo and can't seem to take his eyes off of his Grandma Fannie getting a fair amount of attention from the fuss she's making about imitation meat and bean bowls. Having the other family members stealing all of the attention is rubbing Terri the wrong way.

"So, I guess I'm invisible now. I don't see no cameras on me. If it wasn't for me all of y'all would be still sitting in Camden," Terri claims half-jokingly.

"Oh Lord, here we go," Darcy playfully injects.

"How 'bout putting one of 'em cameras on me. Shit, I'm the one who filled out the survey. There's more to me than these earrings and this blonde hair. I got dreams too," Terri nods to the cameras.

Back in Washington, in the Oval Office, President Wheeler, Nick and a handful of White House staffers are watching the ending of the Family Time Burgers first live TV commercial with the Lantern family while discussing the President's reelection campaign strategy.

"I really liked that one kid's tattoo but I can't be seen with that family. That'll piss off the base," President Wheeler says with a twisted grin.

President Wheeler playfully slaps his right butt cheek then coolly nods to one of his younger staffers to join in, which she smartly doesn't. The President awkwardly shifts his butt then slaps his left butt cheek.

"They say it's all about that base," President Wheeler jokes.

Teasingly, the young staffer and everyone else in the room shake their heads in disbelief at the President's sometimes dry sense of humor.

"And they say I'm out of touch, not woke. Com'on," President Wheeler says with a shrug.

"On the contrary, Mister President, instead of avoiding the meet and greet in Saint Louis with this um..um..colorful family, let's take the upper hand and use this opportunity to get some votes and endorsements from minorities from every state.

"Exactly how many minority endorsements do we have right now, Nick?", President Wheeler asks.

"Actually, sir, we currently have zero"

"That's not good."

"Not good at all, sir."

One of the White House staffers glances at his wristwatch, "Mister President, in about two minutes you have a scheduled private sit down with Senator Bell.

President Wheeler seems perplexed, a bit confused about who exactly is this Senator Bell. The group of staffers walk near the door to leave.

"Sir, I believe he's that new freshman Senator who authored that new bill about dress and hairstyle codes in our public schools. It's all over the news," Nick elaborates while stepping towards the door to leave.

President Wheeler stands with a puzzled face as the door opens. Sharply-dressed Adam, a twenty-something Caucasian intern appears in the doorway escorting the equally-posh, young African-American Senator Bell into the Oval Office. Adam greets the leaving White House staffers and Nick with a cordial, professional nod.

Adam steps slightly forward as the dapper Senator politely stand aside.

"Mister President, Senator Bell," Adam nods.

President Wheeler immediately extends his hand to Adam, the young Caucasian intern.

"Glad to meet you, Senator," the President warmly greets Adam.

Avoiding the President's handshake, Adam quickly turns toward the Senator.

"No, no, sir. This is Senator Bell. I'm Adam. I've been a White House intern here for nearly a year now," Adam explains as Senator Bell sighs at the President's naivety.

I like reading a lot and learning about different things but having this autism thing gets kind of crazy and confusing sometimes. My doctor at the clinic in town says that autism can be good and bad at the same time sometimes. I always listen real close to every word somebody says when they're talking and when I read stuff I read every little word. My doctor says that maybe I shouldn't take everything I read and take everything that people say so seriously all 'the time. My doctor says that people don't always mean what they say and that's why I shouldn't take things so literally all 'the time. But then that's when I get all confused 'cause if people don't mean what they say then maybe they should just shut up and be quiet.

I used to read in the news magazines all the time about how President Wheeler don't like Black people. My father says that some people got so much hate in them against Black people that they can't even hide it even if they got the whole world watching them. My father says that one time when he was driving this big-time general around on base the general had called him 'boy', like he had no rank at all or didn't even deserved to be in the Army, so my father pretended that the jeep had broken down so that the general had to walk almost a mile back to his quarters. My father says that people like President Wheeler should never be in the White House 'cause we can't go nowhere, especially can't go forward when we got backward-minded people in charge of things. Dad says that we'll always be stuck in the 1950's if we keep electing backward-minded people.

Looking somewhat uncomfortable, Senator Bell extends his hand to President Wheeler as Adam politely leaves the Oval Office. There's an awkward silence filling the room as the President motions the young Senator to take a seat.

≼┼≽

CHAPTER 6
SPLENDID BEAUTY

The presidential race is heating up. One particular opponent of President Wheeler is getting a lot of attention and the recent polls shows that she has a good chance of beating him. As a female candidate she's bombarded with constant radio and TV interview requests.

Tonight, in New York City, a live taping of the highly popular talk show 'Late Night with Sonny Connors' is already in progress. The studio audience sits attentively as the host, former stand-up comedian Sonny Connors, engage in a lively conversation with tonight's special guest, presidential candidate Senator April Taylor.

"So, tell us Senator, when was the exact moment when you decided to run for president?", Sonny asks.

"Oh, that's easy, the moment President Wheeler was elected," Senator Taylor quickly replies.

The studio audience erupts with applause as Senator Taylor pleasingly nods at the crowd's reaction.

"Wow, that early?", Sonny asks with a touch of amazement.

※━━※

"Look, ever since his first campaign and now while this man has been in the White House, all we've seen is the ugliness of certain politicians and the ugly side of America. As a parent and a proud American, just like all of you, I want to remind the American people of the splendid beauty of our great country. As a mother, I think that our kids deserve better. President Wheeler represents everything we teach our kids not to do, and I imagine that his upcoming State of the Union address is going to be filled with his typical condescending rhetoric that belittles people," Senator Taylor answers with conviction in her voice.

As the audience explodes with a rousing applause, Sonny motions two stage hands to bring out the stage props of oversized, red boxing gloves and a life-size, cardboard cutout of President Wheeler.

"Senator, our producers did a little research and found out that boxing is your favorite form of exercise and that you actually have a boxing gym in your home. So, for a bit of fun, we thought you wouldn't mind going a few rounds with President Wheeler," Sonny laughs.

Amused, the studio audience chuckle as the two stage hands assists Senator Taylor with slipping on her big red boxing gloves, and then quickly dash to help Sonny with positioning his arms through the armholes of the President Wheeler cardboard cutout.

Genuinely enjoying the skit, Senator Taylor playfully waves to the cheering audience with her oversized gloves, and then, suddenly, she wastes no time delivering a hard left hook that knocks 'cardboard President Wheeler' to the floor!

The audience explodes with laughter and applause as Sonny comically wiggle his legs in the air while lying on his back.

———

Meanwhile, back in Camden, on Ferry Avenue, the Devils are up to something shady. An old beat-up Toyota Camry is slowly cruising down Ferry. Everybody knows when the Devils 'be driving by 'cause they always use those fake dealer tags that's made from paper. The Camry slows to a crawl in front of the Lantern's house as four heads turn, casing the house to ensure that no one is in the house. Not coming to a complete stop, the Camry takes another trip around the block at a snail's pace.

Two houses from the Lantern's home, Mister Red Coles is alone in his living room tapping his feet to the country beat of Linda Martell's 1969 summer hit 'Color Him Father'. As he taps his feet, Red still can't wrap his head around the fact that a Black woman is actually singing this great song.

———

Enjoying the cool breeze coming through an open window, Red sits comfortably in his lazy boy recliner as the CD player fills the room with old Southern memories, some good memories, and some hard memories, the kind of hard memories that sometimes you just want to forget but you can't because you can't seem to shake them off.

As the song plays, Red begins to stare at a framed picture of his estranged daughter resting atop an end table across the room. Apparently, this '69 country hit has dug up something deep inside of Red that's probably been eating at him for years. Red's feet are no longer tapping to the beat. Tears begin to trickle down Red's cheeks as the song continue to echo throughout the room.

Red's memory begins to drift, taking him back to the day when he came home from work and walked into his house to see an eighteen-year-old Black guy sitting at the kitchen table eating a sandwich. Unaware that this young man is his daughter's high school friend, and not realizing that she is in the bathroom, Red immediately begins to berate this young man, calling him a 'nigger' and demanding that he get the hell out of his house right now! When Red's daughter heard all of the commotion in the kitchen she flew out of the bathroom, but when she looked into the kitchen she was pissed to see that he was gone. It took only three quick minutes for Red's daughter to pack the few items that she needed. When she left out the door that evening it was the last time Red saw his daughter.

The song fades. The living room is quiet again. Red wipes the tears from his cheeks. The music has stopped but Red's old memories and regrets linger on.

Suddenly, Red hears voices. Red peeps out the window and sees the rundown Toyota Camry with the fake dealer tags parked curbside in front of the Lantern's house. Red sees four shadowy figures creeping through the Lantern's yard then making their way towards the rear of the house.

Hastily, Red grabs his shotgun from his bedroom closet then hurries out the door!

Moments later, Red catches the four Devils trying to pry open the Lantern's back door.

With Red's shotgun barrel mere inches away from their shocked faces, the Devils freeze.

America: No Purchase Necessary

"I understand how you fellas might have some beef with me but after all 'the stuff Fannie do for everybody in this neighborhood, I don't understand how y'all can come around here and try to break in this kind lady's home! And do what? Steal something?," Red angrily lectures while shaking his head in disgust. Reluctantly, the four Devils walk away without a word.

My mama told me a long time ago to not trust anything that came in pretty packages. My mama got a problem with people who always wear nice suits, like the big government people in Washington. The rotten stuff that President Wheeler 'be doing sometimes reminds me of the same stuff the Devils 'be doing in Camden. I guess when you use people and try to steal stuff when you're wearing a nice suit maybe they call it a different name so people don't think it's something dirty going on. My mama says that business people and politicians wearing them nice shiny suits know how to make dirty stuff look clean.

I'm just eleven now and I can't vote yet but after what President Wheeler did to Rico at his 'State of the Union' speech, I know that I could never vote for him 'cause he steals just like the Camden Devils.

In Washington, DC tonight, on Capitol Hill, it's a special night to bring the nation together. At the House of Representatives, the massive chamber is filled with a mixture of facial expressions, faces of adulation and faces of disdain, among the seated politicians listening to the closing of the State of the Union address as President Wheeler stand firm at the glossy podium delivering his speech with the help of a teleprompter.

News reporters and TV cameras are everywhere. The Vice President and the sneering Speaker of the House are seated behind the President as he speaks to the nation.

"America has certainly been through the mire many times. But you know what, we, as a nation, never stay down long," President Wheeler sternly proclaims while reading the teleprompter.

President Wheeler momentarily takes his eyes off of the teleprompter then slips his hand into his right coat pocket to retrieve a folded note. The President calmly unfolds the note then begins to read the note aloud.

The President takes a deep breath then surprises everyone by speaking in Japanese, "Nana korobi ya oki."

Puzzled faces and gasps spread throughout the packed chamber. Along the chamber left wall, White House press secretary Misty Madsen frantically scans the hardcopy pages of the President's prepared State of the Union speech.

―⟵⊹⟶―

Totally unconcerned with whoever might be watching her, Misty loses control as she shakes her head in frustration at the President going off-script.

"What the fuck?!," Misty sighs.

All heads and network cameras turn their focus on Misty as she furiously tosses the hardcopy speech pages into the air then storms out of the chamber!

Nonchalantly, President Wheeler finishes his speech, "Yes, America, we will fall down sometimes, but with strong borders and good American citizens, we will always get back up."

Still in shock from hearing the President speak in Japanese, the entire chamber is collectively baffled. Awkwardly, the chamber falls completely silent. There's no applause whatsoever as everyone turns to the person next to them asking, "What?"

President Wheeler turns around to face the Speaker of the House who is trying her best to refrain from laughing. Not a big supporter of the President, the Speaker of the House sarcastically says, "Good job, Mister President, good job."

―⟵⊹⟶―

The Lantern family have been on the road, traveling westward on Interstate 70, for a few days. They are on the outskirts of Terre Haute, Indiana parked at a truck stop. The early morning sun is breaking through the clouds as the highway traffic picks up along the busy interstate. The massive truck stop lot is filled with 18-wheelers, Greyhound buses, U-haul trucks, RV's and highway travelers.

In the right corner of the rear lot, the Lantern's eye-catching, big red, white and blue RV is surrounded by an ever-growing mob of News reporters, TV camera crews, photographers, newfound fans of the Lanterns and a steady flow of curious onlookers.

Ever since we did our first live TV commercial in Dayton, a lot of people 'been talking about us in the news, in the papers, on TV, on the radio, everywhere.

No matter where we go or where we stop at now, people wanna see us and sometimes they wanna talk to us. I guess to other people we're somebody now, I guess. I always been just me, so I always been somebody.

My brother and sister like all of this attention we're getting but I just like seeing the different places and towns we 'be passing. Some of the places we've passed I'd already read about on books and magazines. It's kind of fun to see these places for real. My doctor says that I tend to like things and places rather than being around people. I guess that's true, especially when I was younger.

Now, I don't mind doing stuff like telling stories in front of the whole class 'cause when I'm talking sometimes I feel like I'm inside my story and not in the classroom at all.

When I was six my father thought that I was crazy 'cause he was trying to teach me about fixing cars and one day he was standing by the car wearing a shirt that had a big ol' grease spot on it, and in the middle of this big greasy stain there was a small hole that looked like a small mouth, and every time my father would try to talk me about different wrenches and different parts of the motor I would start laughing 'cause I kept looking at the tiny mouth in the middle of the greasy stain and it looked like it was talking to me.

My father didn't think anything about it was funny though. He got real mad and told my mother that I probably 'wasn't right upstairs'.

I've been going to the clinic for a long time now. My doctor says that I got ASD. It's short for autism spectrum disorder, but one day I made my doctor laugh real hard 'cause I told him that if I really got this ASD thing, then it probably means 'awesome special dude'.

I still don't like a whole lot of people around like Terri and Latoya do though. They really like all the cameras, photographers, and reporters. We've been stuck in Camden for so long, I think 'I just like watching my family have some real fun for a change.

In the corner of the gigantic truck stop, the Lanterns' colorful RV has drawn quite a crowd. Inside the spacious RV, most of the family is still asleep. Cloaked in plaid pajamas, Ronnie steps out of the restroom with a curious expression as he faintly hears muffled crowd noise. Ronnie walks toward the front of the RV and quietly peeps through the lower corner of the windshield blinds.

Ronnie sees the large gathering of reporters, fans and looky loos anxiously awaiting the family to step out of the RV.

Hurriedly, Ronnie dash down the hallway to Terri's room. Being careful not to awaken the rest of the family, Ronnie softly knocks on Terri's door.

"Terri?", Ronnie softly knocks again.

Behind the closed door, Terri is half-dressed and lying on his back silently reading a book entitled, 'Becoming a Lawyer.'

"Terri? You woke?", Ronnie softly whispers from the hallway.

Terri hastily buries the book underneath the blanket then sits up.

"Ronnie? Com'on in," Terri says while wiping the tiredness out of his eyes from the hours of reading.

Ronnie steps in with excitement on his face, "Terri, you gotta see this. Com'on."

Ronnie leads Terri down the hallway towards the front to take a peek at the growing crowd outside.

Quietly, Ronnie gestures Terri to peep through the lower corner of the windshield blinds. Terri peeks.

"Aww shit. We 'famous now. We gotta get everybody up. It's show time," Terri says with his confident swag.

A short time later, the elated crowd of reporters and fans outside the Lantern's RV burst into cheer and applause as the yawning Lanterns slowly step out of the luxury mobile home still draped in their comfortable sleepwear and pajamas.

Ronnie, Latoya, Rico, Grandma Fannie, Darcy, and Reggie are all standing alongside the RV awaiting Terri's exit. All eyes and news cameras are fixated on the RV door.

Stylishly dressed, Terri finally appears at the doorway striking a pose in full makeup. The crowd responds with a pleasing cheer.

Every news reporter and journalist are anxious to ask the family a few questions. An ABC News reporter takes the lead, "Good morning to you all and congratulations. How does it feel to be 'America's Family'?"

Sleepy-eyed and shamelessly yawning again, Grandma Fannie, Reggie, Darcy, Rico and Latoya all begin to stretch while Ronnie wipes his eyes as the early morning sun begins to shine. Terri, on the other hand, is eager and more than ready to answer any questions.

"Y'all gotta forgive them. We've been on the road and they ain't never been nowhere before," Terri teases.

In unison, Grandma Fannie, Darcy, Reggie, Rico, Latoya and Ronnie turn their heads and shoot Terri a look as the amused crowd smiles admiringly at the family's comradery and playfulness.

Terri straightens his posture then gets serious as he speaks to the crowd and the numerous TV cameras, "For real though, coming from Camden, New Jersey, it feels good to be recognized for something really positive for a change."

Collectively, the crowd nods pleasingly at Terri's comments.

A reporter from NBC News looks directly at Rico, "I have a question for you Rico. Um, Rico, what did you think of the President's State of the Union address when he spoke in Japanese and basically repeated the exact message on your tattoo?"

Immediately, the Lanterns come to Rico's defense as their disdain and bitterness towards President Wheeler is revealed on national TV. Grandma Fannie's face twist and cringe as she interjects her true feelings, "I'm telling y'all right now, that Wheeler ain't no good. He's low down and dirty! I'm telling y'all."

Reggie chimes in, "You know, the least he could've done is tell Rico ahead of time that he was going to mention the message on Rico's tattoo in his speech."

Darcy steps forward, "And we already heard on the news that President Wheeler never ever set one foot in Japan in his whole entire life so we know for sure 'he stole it from seeing Rico's tattoo in that live commercial we did."

"And when we meet President Wheeler in St. Louis, we gotta few things we wanna get straight with him," Latoya adds.

An ABC News reporter notices Rico blushing at the Lanterns' love and support. The reporter asks, "Rico, is there anything that you would like to add?"

Without hesitation, Rico raises his right forearm and proudly displays his tattoo written in Japanese characters, then utters, "Yeah, I would like to say something. First of all, I wear this tattoo with all my heart because my father served in the military at Kadena Air Force Base in Okinawa Japan and he used to write me letters all the time telling me stuff about the cool things he'd learned over there."

Rico's face is consumed with emotion. The entire crowd is captivated. Rico has their complete and undivided attention. Rico sighs then continues, "And then when my father finished his tour in Japan he got deported back to Mexico because they said that his papers weren't finalized or some crazy shit like that, and then they said that he wasn't a legal American citizen. So, like I said, I wear this tattoo for my father, for my mother in heaven, and for all the other hardworking people out there who love this country but were deported for all the wrong reasons." And then Rico gestures with a pointed finger, signaling to the crowd that he's about to speak in Japanese, "Nana korobi ya oki."

Momentarily, the crowd is speechless until a CBS News reporter breaks the silence, "Hey Terri, can you tell us what you plan to do with the sweepstakes prize money?"

"Most of it is going to cover tuition and books for my paralegal classes, and then, hopefully, law school," Terri answers.

It wasn't Terri's blonde hair or dangling earrings that grabbed everyone's attention this time. This time, it was Terri's intellect and ambition that had jaws dropping and heads turning. Even Terri's own mother was caught off-guard.

Darcy turns to Terri with a puzzled face, "Law school?"

"Law school," Terri nods assuredly.

Abruptly, a middle age woman hastily waves her hand above the crowd while cutting in between the TV cameras and reporters. The woman seems to be eyeing Grandma Fannie as she reaches the front of the crowd.

"I have a question for Fannie. I saw you on TV talking about beans. Do you have a special way you do your beans?", the woman asks.

"Sure. I make different kinds but here's a real easy one for you. All you gotta do is boil some navy beans 'til they're nice and soft and then you chop some broccoli real fine and add them to the beans with a little salt and pepper and the last thing you're going to add a touch of lemon juice and then that's it. Mmmm, simple and so good," Grandma Fannie nods with a smile.

The woman is having trouble following and remembering Grandma Fannie's instructions but she pretends she's got it with a polite face, "Okay, thanks."

Not too far from Washington, DC and a short distance from the headquarters of the Family Time

Corporation in Fairfax, Virginia, the Pine Hill Golf Course and Country Club has become a favorite meeting place for politicians, lobbyists and business people as they make deals over lunch and sometimes over a round of golf.

At the back nine on this pristine green, six observant Secret Service agents are standing guard a short distance away as President Wheeler plays a round of golf with his biggest campaign donor, Jake Astor.

President Wheeler studies the trajectory of his next shot as Jake looks on with a pompous grin.

"You know Dennis, your game's been off lately," Jake injects.

"It's that damn Lantern family, Jake. That sweepstakes contest wasn't supposed to turn out like that. And now they're hounding me about that Mexican kid's tattoo," President Wheeler sighs.

"Dennis, I hope you realize that you're using a putter instead of a five iron on that shot. But don't let me mess up your game," Jake says with a sarcastic grin.

President Wheeler sighs then quickly exchanges clubs from his golf bag propped alongside their cart. Again, the President grabs the wrong golf club for his particular shot, but this time, Jake doesn't say anything.

"Jake, maybe we should call this whole thing off," President Wheeler suggests.

"Dennis, now calm down. A deal's a deal. Business is business. I know we told Nick it's all done on a handshake but remember we actually got papers on this deal. I don't do anything this big without papers. Besides, I already bank rolled your reelection Super Bowl ad, and honestly, I'm in way too deep with you and this 'America's Family' deal," Jake lectures.

President Wheeler tightens his lips then releases his frustration with a hard swing at his golf ball. The President ponders while eyeing the ball take flight.

Jake continues with his thoughts about his current deal with the President, "Dennis, just like what we'd agreed to, I say you do the meet and greet with the Lantern family in Saint Louis and you just put on a good show like you always do."

At first the grownups try to teach us kids that stuff like stealing and lying is wrong but then they go and do it themselves. Sometimes I don't always agree with what Monica says 'cause sometimes I think that she really might hurt somebody, but when she says that maybe we should let the kids vote and let the kids run things sometimes I think maybe we should try it out and see what happens 'cause the sneaky stuff that President Wheeler 'be doing just ain't right. And when my grandma would talk about the snakes in Washington I know now why she says those things.

While absorbing Jake's suggestions and watching his ball land on the green far from the hole, mischievous thoughts enter the President's head.

President Wheeler turns to Jake with a peculiar look, "But what if the Lanterns don't make it to Saint Louis?"

Momentarily Jake is dumbfounded, then obviously confused, "Don't make it to Saint Louis?"

President Wheeler responds with a crooked smile then motions one of his security agents to come closer.

The President whispers something into the agent's ear as Jake looks on with cautious eyes.

CHAPTER 7
BRITTANY'S WAY

Everyone knows that a lot of dirty politics and shady back door deals are going on in Washington, and many reporters and journalists knows this as well but have made a choice to look away and pretend it doesn't exist. But New York World reporter Brittany Stills takes her job seriously, and she has smelled something fishy since the day that President Wheeler was elected and she's determined to expose his dirty deeds and shady deals.

In the parking lot of the Family Time Corporation Headquarters, a shiny blue Ford Fusion is slowly maneuvering through the near-capacity lot then crawls to a stop near a parked rusty, red Chevy Impala.

The blue Ford pulls into the empty spot next to the beat-up Impala.

Looking around suspiciously, Brittany Stills steps out of the blue Ford then quickly slides into the passenger seat of the red Impala.

Sitting anxiously behind the wheel of the Chevy Impala is thirty-year-old Valerie, one of the many Latinas and Asian janitorial workers at the lofty Family Time Headquarters building.

Wearing her required American flag-themed red, white and blue janitorial vest, Valerie greets Brittany in her best English.

⸺

"You 'Brittany?", Valerie asks.

"Yes. Are you Valerie?"

Valerie nods 'yes' then begins to remove her colorful janitorial vest.

"You bring money?", Valerie asks.

Brittany digs up a hundred-dollar bill out of her jean pocket then hands it to Valerie. In return, Valerie hands Brittany her flag-themed janitor's vest and her set of master keys.

Struggling with her English, Valerie further instructs Brittany, "You get yo' paper. Maybe you 'find it in desk drawer. I don't know, but you must clean third floor bathrooms. My job is third floor toilets. Me have no job if toilets no clean."

Brittany slips on the colorful vest then stuffs the master key set into her vest pocket.

Brittany gives Valerie a reassuring nod, "Got it. No problem, Valerie. I'll make sure that the third floor restrooms are nice and clean. But what if somebody looks at me and see that it's not you?"

Valerie chuckles at Brittany's naivete, then explains, "That'll never happen. We 'in the vest is invisible to them. They look right through us. We 'nothing to them. We clean. That's it. Just clean. We 'nobody."

"And Mister Jake Astor's office?", Brittany injects with determined eyes.

"Top floor," Valerie nods.

A few minutes later, the hallway on the tenth floor is somewhat quiet. Wrapped in the flag-themed vest, Brittany steps off of the elevator with her yellow janitor's cart then speedily walks down the elaborate corridor ornamented with fancy carpet, ritzy decor and gold-trim glass doors.

Brittany quietly rolls her cart near a spacious conference room occupied with Jake Astor and his marketing and sales team.

The conference room gold-trim glass door is partially open. Cautiously, Brittany watches an executive standing next to a weekly sales graph showing slow sales of their new veggie burger and a contrasting, highlighted area labeled in bold letters 'Potential Sales of Grandma Fannie's Bean Bowls'.

Brittany eavesdrops as the marketing executive explains her strategy to Jake Astor and the rest of the team, "If we offer her sixty percent and put her sweet grandmotherly face on all of the different varieties of her bean bowls we would giving our customers another alternative to our veggie burgers, and possibly, that could increase the sales of both. Good for our customers, good for Family Time, it's a win-win for everybody."

Brittany slowly moves on, quietly pushing her yellow cart down the elaborate corridor. Inconspicuously, she glances at the various executives' door plaques along the lengthy hallway then suddenly stops at the gold-trim door labeled 'CEO Jake Astor'.

Not wasting time, Brittany uses the master key, enters the vacant office and swiftly whips out her cellphone from her back pocket then quickly snaps a picture of the framed wall photo of President Wheeler and Jake Astor holding golf clubs.

As a dedicated investigative reporter, Brittany is focused on finding the dirt and underhanded connection between the President and Jake Astor. Brittany hastily opens the bottom left drawer of Jake's glossy desk then hurriedly scan the file tabs. Nothing grabs her attention. In a flash, Brittany shifts and opens the bottom right drawer then rapidly thumbs through the file tabs and abruptly stops midway through the numerous folders.

A triumphant grin surfaces on Brittany's face as she yanks out a folder from the drawer then removes a signed, two-page contract agreement, which links President Wheeler to the Family Time Corporation 'America's Family' Sweepstakes for a payment of three million dollars, out of the folder.

Methodically, Brittany lays the contract agreement flat atop the desk then quickly snaps a picture of the first page with her cellphone then swiftly flips the first sheet to take a photo of the second page.

Rapidly, Brittany shoves the letter back into the folder then stuffs the folder back into the drawer.

Satisfied, Brittany grabs her yellow janitor's cart then heads to the door to leave.

Moments later, Brittany is in the elevator. No one else is in the elevator. The third-floor button is lit. Standing alongside her cleaning cart, Brittany is headed down to the third-floor to clean the bathrooms and keep her promise to Valerie. To Brittany's surprise, the elevator suddenly stops at the fifth-floor. The door opens and Johnny, wearing the cleaning staff flag-themed vest, enters with his yellow cart.

Immediately, Johnny's lustful eyes begin to examine Brittany's curves as she politely moves her cart to make room in the elevator.

Johnny presses the first-floor button while slyly stealing glances at Brittany's shapely body.

Brittany notices Johnny's lustful side-glances. Smartly, Brittany sets a plan in motion to take care of the promise she'd made to Valerie. Coolly, Brittany unbuttons the top button of her blouse to showcase more of her enticing cleavage.

"Are you new here?", Johnny asks as his eyes gaze Brittany's seductive breasts.

"Yup, and they got me running around here doing all this stuff today. I got to do all the bathrooms on three and this other stuff too after that. I don't know how I'm going to get time for my break," Brittany sighs while conspicuously eyeing Johnny to see if he fell for it.

And just as she expected, Johnny takes the bait.

"Hey, I got a few minutes. I can knock out the third-floor bathrooms for you right now and then maybe we can catch lunch together later," Johnny smoothly suggests.

Slyly, Brittany shifts her alluring cleavage for a better view for Johnny.

"That'll be great. I'll knock out this other stuff and then we could meet up later," Brittany nods convincingly.

A few minutes later, with absolutely no intentions of meeting up with Johnny, Brittany is in the parking lot. Immediately, Brittany heads straight towards Valerie's car. Brittany taps on the driver side window of the rundown Chevy Impala. Valerie winds down the window. Brittany hands the colorful janitor's vest and the master key set to Valerie.

In her unique broken English, Valerie asks, "You 'clean toilets?"

"Mission accomplished," Brittany coolly nods.

Brittany is all smiles as she slides into her blue Ford Fusion and leaves the parking lot.

My sister Latoya got that kind of beauty that don't need a whole lot of makeup. My sister's biggest dream is to be on magazine covers and TV one day but she's always fussy about her hair though. One day, me and

Latoya was the only ones at home. We were just laying around doing nothing and then my sister asked me to cut her hair 'cause she said that she had too many split ends. At first, I didn't know what she meant when she said split ends but now I know though.

Right now, I think that America got too many split ends too. Ever since President Wheeler have been in charge it's like the whole country is split, even people in the same family is split up too. And even though he's the President right now, President Wheeler's family ain't no different from anybody else's family 'cause they got split ends too. And my sister says that when you got split ends you got to cut them off so that the hair can grow back stronger.

But, you know, sometimes I don't know though, as I think about it more and more, maybe President Wheeler actually might got more split ends in his family than everybody else.

It's a week night and it's getting late at the Family Time Burgers conveniently located at the Metro Center in Washington, DC. At the corner of Twelveth and 'G' Street, metro riders and local teens fill the bustling hangout every evening with its trademarked patriotic decor and flag-themed tabletops. There's a steady flow of patrons going in and out from the carry-out register as three waitresses greet and seat the dine-in customers at the tables and booths along the windows facing the street.

President Wheeler's purple-hair, sixteen-year-old, free-spirited daughter Emily is sharing a basket of fried onion rings at a cozy booth with her best friend Deon, the teen son of a prominent Nigerian diplomat. It's obvious that the flirtatious way Emily looks at Deon that this friendship is beyond platonic.

Emily has a ten-inch white bandage covering a fresh tattoo on her right forearm.

Three tables away, two Secret Service agents are sipping on a cup of coffee while keeping a watchful eye on Emily.

Emily is anxious to see her new tattoo. She slowly peels back the corner of the bandage.

"Emily, don't! It needs to stay wrapped longer. Remember?", Deon warns.

Ignoring Deon, Emily slowly peels off the entire bandage, revealing a series of Japanese characters, the same tattoo Rico had revealed on national TV and seemingly has become extremely popular among teenagers all across the country. With a telling gaze, Deon's chocolate hand softly caps Emily's fingers then gently guide and reapply the bandage back over the tattoo with her hand.

One of the Secret Service agents is speaking on his cellphone to someone at the White House while the other agent shifts his eyes squarely on Deon's dark brown hand touching Emily's pale skin.

A young couple sits at the nearby booth. The waitress takes their order.

With a warm perky smile, the waitress delivers her best sales pitch for Family Time's latest menu item to the young couple, "Would you like to try our new Grandma Fannie's Bean Bowl with that? We got eight different types. Ranch. Spicy. They're half-price for the rest of the month."

"Sure, I'll have one. Ranch, please" the young lady politely nods.

"Me too. Ranch. I heard that they're pretty tasty," the young man says with hungry eyes.

With their eyes glued on Deon and the President's daughter, the agent with the cellphone buries it then nonchalantly walks to Emily's booth.

"Emily, we need to wrap this up. Your father wants to see you right now," the agent says with a no-nonsense expression.

Emily shoots the button-down agent a scornful eye as she and Deon reluctantly scoots out of the booth.

⇌

A short time later, at the White House, there's a familiar chill permeating in President Wheeler's bedroom.

Cladded in posh pajamas, President Wheeler and the First Lady are avoiding each other as the President quietly sits at a small desk, on the right side of the spacious elegant room, indifferently scanning through the headlines of the New York Times and The Washington Post.

The First Lady is across the room pouring herself a nightcap at the luxurious mini bar conveniently adjacent to their big empty bed.

A broad, wall-mounted TV is broadcasting the CNN Late News but no one is watching or listening to it. Whether it's alcohol, newspapers or the TV, the Wheelers seemingly would use anything to avoid talking to each other.

On the TV screen, the CNN News anchor runs through a quick summary of today's events with brief corresponding images popping up on the screen related to the story.

On the wide screen, to the left of the anchor, an image appears of the White House Press Secretary Misty Madsen with a bold 'X' covering her mouth.

The CNN News anchor reports, "Earlier this evening White House Press Secretary Misty Madsen was disrupted and then willingly left a restaurant in her hometown of Frederick, Maryland as a group of angry patrons repeatedly began chanting 'Potty Mouth Misty!' as she dined with her family."

An image of a tattoo consisting of Japanese characters appears on the TV screen.

The CNN News anchor continues, "And tattoo parlors across the country are seeing the request of one particular tattoo, which was made widely known by Rico from the 'America's Family' live commercial, and then, some say, was subsequently stolen by the President during his State of the Union address. The trendy tattoo translates to 'fall down seven times, get up eight' in English and is especially popular among teenagers.

Separate photo images of President Wheeler and his golf buddy, Jake Astor, appear on the TV screen.

The CNN News anchor goes on to explain, "And, in more White House news, New York World reporter Brittany Stills revealed today that she has concrete evidence that President Wheeler is selling and financially profiting from his title as President of the United States."

Abruptly, from the hallway, the bedroom door swings open.

President Wheeler has been expecting his daughter. He quickly scans his cluttered desk and finds the TV remote. Although the TV news is completely being ignored by the President and his wife, President Wheeler lowers the TV volume as the CNN anchor elaborates on the details of the President's handsome payment from Jake Astor for the President's upcoming appearance in Saint Louis with the 'America's Family' sweepstakes winner.

With the white bandage covering her new tattoo, purple-hair Emily is pissed as she steps into her parent's bedroom.

"You wanted to see me, Dad?", Emily sighs.

President Wheeler rise from his desk as his wife quietly avoids the anticipated confrontation and looks on with a full glass of wine in her hand.

"Emily, honey, you know we don't mind you dating, but being seen with that boy could hurt my reelection chances. You know how the media is," President Wheeler pleads.

"First of all, he's not 'that boy'. His name is Deon. And Dad, why do you keep saying stuff like 'we don't mind you dating blah blah blah blah' when mom don't even think like you do. It wouldn't be Deon's fault if you didn't get reelected. It'll be your own fault.

Even I know that and I'm supposed to be the dumb one," Emily fires back then storms out the door.

Admiring her daughter's spirited gumption, the First Lady smiles then takes a big gulp of her wine. President Wheeler, on the other hand, shakes his head in disgust.

Meanwhile, on Interstate 70, traveling westward near Effingham, Illinois, the Lanterns are continuing their cross-country trip in their luxury RV. Reggie is behind the wheel. Darcy has her bare feet propped up on the dashboard as they cruise through rural Illinois in fairly light traffic.

"This thing sure rides nice and smooth for a big ol' thing. I wonder what Terri's going to do with it after the trip," Darcy glances at Reggie with a curious look.

Unbeknownst to Darcy and Reggie, Terri exits the hallway bathroom then casually steps toward the front of the cruising RV. Darcy and Reggie are still talking about what Terri might do with the fancy RV. Terri eavesdrops, and when he hears his name mentioned he abruptly drops to his hands and knees then quietly creep closer up front to listen to each and every word of his parents' conversation.

Reggie proclaims, "Terri's probably going to give it to me because ----"

"Because what? If he gives it to anybody he'll probably give it to me. Terri loves his mama," Darcy interjects with a knowing smile.

Stooped down and out of his parents' sight, Terri shakes his head in amusement at his parents' carrying on.

"Aw, woman, you're crazy. He loves his pops and he knows that ever since I used to drive those jeeps and big trucks in the Army, and all I used to talk about is quitting the factory and running my own business. I could start my own bus tour," Reggie nods.

"In Camden? Who wanna see Camden?"

"Camden got some good parts."

"Where?"

Darcy laughs as Reggie sighs.

"Besides, Terri likes me better. Remember when he was fourteen and that day he came out to us?", Darcy asks as her mind drifts to a few years ago.

Still quietly hunched over and out of his parents' sight, a big loving smile spreads across Terri's face as he continually eavesdrops on their conversation.

Darcy chuckles lightly as she reminisces, "He was so cute and so nervous."

Reggie giggles then adds, "Remember when he finished and just stood there all scared like he was about to wet his pants? And then we told him we'd already known."

"How could we not know, especially when he was stealing my red lipstick ever since he was ten," Darcy interjects.

Still hiding behind his parents' seats, Terri teasingly corrects his mother, "It wasn't red. It was scarlet crimson."

Totally surprised, Darcy turns around as Terri springs up and joins his loving parents in playful laughter.

Meanwhile, further down the hallway in Latoya's room, Rico is standing next to the window as the Illinois countryside rolls by. The afternoon sunlight illuminates the tattoo of Japanese characters along Rico's forearm as he talks on his cellphone with his father in Mexico.

Latoya is sitting up on her bed daydreaming of a glamorous Hollywood life as she gazes at the beautiful faces and shapely bodies on the glossy pages of Vogue magazine.

Rico is saying goodbye to his father, "Love you too, Dad...Oh, she's right here on the bed with some dude. And get this, Dad. She's asking me to leave the room to give them some privacy."

Latoya playfully tosses her magazine at Rico as he hands his cellphone to her.

Teasingly, Latoya gives Rico a scornful eye while speaking on the phone, "Hey, Mister Garcia. I wish you was here to teach your son how to be a gentleman. I think the only reason I put up with him is because he's your son."

Amused, Rico cracks a smile while looking out the window.

"And Mister Garcia, me and Rico are emailing immigration agencies and politicians just about every day trying to get somebody to respond and help you get back here...Love you too. Bye."

Latoya places the cellphone atop a small nightstand then looks at Rico as he gazes out the window watching the serene countryside go by. Latoya knows that Rico is deeply hurting inside as his father is so far away. She's old enough to know that Rico needs real comfort right now, true intimacy, which is something she's been struggling with, and this is something that's been weighing on her for quite some time now. Watching Rico peer out the window, Latoya gently gives Rico a reassuring tap on his shoulder. She knows that the comforting tap is not enough but that's all that she can give.

A short distance further down the hallway, the kitchenette is where the oldest and the youngest member of the Lantern family spend some of their time on this cross-country journey.

Always craving knowledge, young Ronnie is sitting at the scaled down dining table reading the latest issue of New York World magazine with a cover photo of President Wheeler and an eye-catching caption in bold, red letters reading 'AVAILABLE FOR BOOKINGS'.

An empty paper plate and a plastic spoon are placed on the table in front of Ronnie as his Grandma Fannie sprinkle spices into a small sauce pan of simmering navy beans atop the stove.

Cloaked in a colorful apron, Grandma Fannie spoons out a small serving of beans then places it on Ronnie's plate. Calmly, Grandma Fannie stands over Ronnie and awaits his trusted feedback.

Ronnie puts his magazine aside then takes a taste of the seasoned beans. Seemingly, Ronnie and Grandma Fannie have been through these routines countless times before. Ronnie slowly chews and throws the beans around in his mouth before taking a swallow as Grandma Fannie patiently stands by with folded arms.

"Grandma, I think you need to cut back on the cayenne pepper 'cause it's too pronounced and drowning out that hint of cinnamon," Ronnie says with confidence.

"Pronounced? Hm, are you sure you're Reggie's kid? I never heard my Reggie ever using big words like that," Grandma Fannie playfully teases.

Ronnie gets back to reading his New York World magazine as Grandma Fannie plants a tender 'thank you' kiss on his cheek for his gifted taste-testing skills.

"Alright, baby. I guess I can't win 'em all, but I for sure thought I had a winner with that one," Grandma Fannie sighs.

―――

Later that day, along the left side of the Flying J Travel Center massive parking lot in Effingham, Illinois, sweepstakes coordinator Sherry Will stands next to her stylish 2020 Mercedes-Benz GLE awaiting the Lantern family's arrival.

The Lanterns' extravagant RV exits Interstate 70 then enters the crowded lot of the vibrant travel center.

Sherry spots the flag-colored RV and begins to wildly wave her arms to get Reggie's attention.

Reggie parks the RV near Sherry's Mercedes. Sherry retrieves two, fully-packed mail bags from the back of her ritzy Benz.

Moments later, in the spacious living room of the Lanterns' RV, the two stuffed mail bags sit in front of Sherry as she touches base and briefs the entire family on their next live TV commercial and meeting with President Wheeler in St. Louis.

"Hey guys, America's really loving this family! I'm so excited! We've been getting great feedback every day through thousands of emails, and as you can see right here, even hundreds of snail mail too. I think you guys maybe becoming more popular than the President," Sherry nods.

Sherry opens the two canvas bags and start to hand out an envelope to each of the family members. Excitedly, Ronnie and Rico begin to dig deeper into the crammed mail bags.

"Grandma, you got a lot of letters in here!", Ronnie says with awestruck eyes.

"Oh, that's right. I almost forgot. Fannie, I got something special for you," Sherry says while digging into her purse and retrieving a check. Sherry happily hands it to Grandma Fannie.

Grandma Fannie's eyes widen in surprise as she glances at the enormous dollar amount on the check.

"That's for sharing your recipes and allowing Family Time Restaurants to sell Grandma Fannie's Bean Bowls across the country," Sherry nods to Fannie then turns to Latoya, "And I don't want to jump the gun here but our marketing department did discuss the idea of Grandma Fannie and her beautiful granddaughter doing a commercial together for the variety of bean bowls," Sherry gives a wink and a nod to Latoya.

Latoya is speechless. She blushes as she absorbs the thought of actually having a role in a real TV commercial.

"Like I said, I don't want to get too far ahead of ourselves here, but I think Family Time has hired a production company already to develop a script for the commercial," Sherry adds as Latoya continues to quietly glow.

Grandma Fannie is still overwhelmed by the large sum on her check.

"This is sure a lot of money," Grandma Fannie says.

"Just save it," Darcy suggests.

Sherry interjects and continues with her briefing, "And hey guys, you've been booked on the 'Your America' talk show when we're out in L.A., and the other thing I wanted to give you a little heads up on is the longer Q and A session with the President in Saint Louis. I believe they're still ironing out the details, possibly having President Wheeler sitting with you guys during the live commercial."

Everyone cringes then shake their heads in disgust as they each imagine sitting at the same table with President Wheeler.

"You know what I'm going to do? I'm going to donate some of this money from my check and send it to that campaign of that real nice lady running against that slimy Wheeler. What's her name?", Grandma Fannie asks.

"Senator April Taylor," Ronnie quickly answers.

"Yep, that's her. This country needs her, especially right now," Grandma Fannie adds.

Sherry is concerned about the Lanterns' dislike of President Wheeler, "Look, I can't tell none of you how to act around the President because, of course, we certainly want everyone to be yourselves. But we, the Family Time Corporation, do hope that everybody will be respectful and cordial towards the President in St. Louis."

Darcy glances at Reggie. Reggie glances at Ronnie. Latoya glances at Rico. Everyone is trying their best to refrain from laughing at Sherry's comment.

"Oh, we'll be cordial alright," Grandma Fannie says with a sarcastic grin.

Collectively, the rest of the family burst into laughter.

Meanwhile, back at the White House, it looks like President Wheeler and his cunning, reelection campaign manager Nick have already launched their sneaky plan to stop the Lanterns from reaching St. Louis.

In the Oval Office, President Wheeler anxiously sits at his desk as snake-tongue Nick hovers closely over his shoulder. Nick's cellphone rests atop the President's desk.

"Nick, if I have to take pictures and hobnob with that family in St. Louis it's going to look bad, really bad. The base will probably all pull out," the President sighs.

"Don't worry, Dennis. The boys got this," Nick nods with confidence.

Calmly, Nick taps the 'speaker' icon on his cellphone resting atop the desk.

Nick speaks to two Secret Service agents looking out for the Lanterns' RV along Interstate 70 somewhere in rural Illinois, "How are we looking fellas?"

Two no-nonsense Secret Service agents sits patiently in a 2020 cold-black Cadillac Escalade on the edge of an old dirt road adjacent to Interstate 70 West.

The agent in the passenger seat responds to Nick by way of his lightweight blue tooth device hooked on his left ear, "No eyes yet, sir."

Five seconds later, the Lanterns' lavish red, white and blue RV cruises along in the flow of traffic headed westward towards St. Louis on Interstate 70.

The agent speaks into his blue tooth, "Sir, we got eyes. We have eyes on the subject. And, for clarification sake, what exactly are we stopping the subjects for?"

While listening to Nick's outlandish response, the rigid agent turns to his partner behind the wheel with a look of utter disbelief then questions Nick again, "Just make up something? Roger that, sir."

⇌

Unaware of the Secret Service agents on their tail, the Lanterns are casually cruising Interstate 70 with Darcy now driving. With both hands tightly on the steering wheel, Darcy keeps her eyes steady on the road while Reggie struggles to keep his eyes open in the passenger seat.

Darcy teases, "Didn't I say not to have those drinks? And you're supposed to be the one operating your own tour bus? Hm."

Reggie fires back, "Aw, look who's talking. You better keep your eyes on the road. You know you can't talk and drive at the same time. See, at least I know my limitations. I don't drive and drink."

Darcy cracks a smile as Reggie's comments triggered some old high school memories.

"Limitations? You're the one who don't know your limitations 'cause if you did you wouldn't had tried to get in Debbie Tims' pants," Darcy chuckles.

"Debbie Tims? Back in high school?"

Darcy gives Reggie a look.

"I don't forget nothing," Darcy teases with a playful smile.

"Woman, you're crazy. And you better keep your eyes on the road 'cause you're talking way too much," Reggie laughs.

Seconds later, Darcy shifts her eyes to her side view mirror and notice that the black Cadillac Escalade is presumably following them.

"Reggie, look in your side mirror. Don't you think that Escalade is little too close?"

Reggie glances at his passenger side mirror. His face turns concerned then he loudly calls out for his oldest son, "Terri! Terri! Com'on up here!"

Firmly clenching the steering wheel, Darcy ease up on the gas and slows the RV as the black Escalade pass and swerves in front of her.

In stylish earrings and freshen lipstick, Terri approaches with curious Ronnie by his side.

"What's up?", Terri asks.

Reggie points to the slow-moving black Escalade directly in front of them, now with its blinking right signal light on, "Terri, did Sherry say anything about this? They've been following us."

"Nope. Nothing 'bout this," Terri shakes his head with baffled eyes.

"Looks like they want us to pull over," Darcy utters.

Ronnie quickly studies the rear of the Escalade as it slows and crawls to a stop along the right shoulder. Ronnie notices that the Escalade don't have license plates.

"That's a government car," Ronnie proclaims.

"Mama, go ahead and pull over behind them. I got this," Terri says with conviction. Both Reggie and Ronnie double-take as they've never heard this level of confidence from Terri before.

Darcy carefully maneuvers the RV along the right shoulder then parks behind the black Escalade.

Traffic along Interstate 70 zooms by as the two dark-suited Secret Service agents exit the Escalade.

The serious-face agents calmly walk towards the right side of the Lanterns' RV then tap on the side entrance door.

Standing in perfect posture with courtroom credence, Terri opens the side door as the rest of the family quietly huddle together behind him in the front living room.

Somewhat awkwardly, the rigid agents try to steer their eyes away from Terri's juicy lips and glistening earrings in the afternoon sun but they can't.

"Good afternoon. We need to take a look inside your vehicle," one of the agents coldly utters.

"Any particular reason why?", Terri asks.

The poker face agents tighten their mouths in response to Terri's audacity to question them.

One of the agents inches forward, "You need to step aside and ---"

Coolly, Terri interrupts, "And what? According to federal rule forty-one you're in violation of proper search and seizure if you can't present probable cause or a warrant."

Taken aback by Terri's legal knowledge, the agents glance at one another, sighs then decide to simply walk away without a single word to Terri.

Impressed with Terri's legal savvy, the rest of the family nod and high-five one another with triumphant smiles in the spacious living room.

Terri shuts the side door then joins the rest of the family. Rico steps forward to shake Terri's hand then jokes, "Hey, Rule Forty-one, I wonder if I can retain your legal services. You see, I got this girlfriend who's always taking shots at my gentleman skills. Can I sue her for pain and suffering?"

Amused, Terri smiles as Latoya gives Rico a hard elbow to his ribs!

"See what I mean?", Rico laughs.

Reggie steps toward Terri.

"No, no, Rule Forty-one. All joking aside, I really need your legal help. I got this wife who's always wrongly accusing me of doing the 'what what' to an ol' high school friend. Can I sue her for pain and suffering? Tell me I got a solid case," Reggie nods to Terri.

Playfully, Darcy shoves Reggie aside then steps towards Terri, "No, no, Rule Forty-one. I got a real case for you."

Teasingly, Darcy shoots Reggie a look then turns to face Terri again.

"Rule Forty-one, I like to hire you as my divorce lawyer so I can finally get rid of this fool," Darcy jokes.

"You know what, I'm gonna have all y'all committed to a mental asylum 'cause y'all 'crazy. Plain straight up crazy," Terri chuckles.

Everyone cracks a smile as Terri takes a brief moment to humbly admire the way he handled himself with the two agents.

Looking through the windshield with an inquisitive eye, Ronnie observes the black Escalade pulling off and merging back into the flow of traffic on Interstate 70 West, towards St. Louis.

Reluctantly, the Secret Service agent in the passenger seat calls the White House to fill Nick and the President in on their failed mission.

In the Oval Office, seated at his lavish desk, President Wheeler sighs in disappointment while listening to his shrewd campaign manager speak into the cellphone atop the desk.

Nick is shaking his head in utter disbelief as he talks to the agents, "Wait, let me see if I understand this correctly. You are two highly-trained, federal agents and you couldn't complete a simple task because you were stopped by --- and these are your exact words --- a transvestite lawyer?"

The Secret Service agent's voice quickly confirms over the cellphone speaker, "Affirmative, sir."

Momentarily, Nick is speechless then sighs, "A transvestite lawyer?"

CHAPTER 8
THE GIFT

Ferry Avenue hasn't been the same ever since the Lantern family have been gone, and no one knows that better than Mister Red Coles. Camden has nicer neighborhoods than the Ferry Avenue area but Red could never afford the pricey homes in Collingswood or Ashland. Red has been living on Ferry Avenue for years but his only true friend on the street is Grandma Fannie.

The Lanterns won't be back in New Jersey until another couple of weeks. The longing to see Fannie again is something that Red's been struggling with for the past few days. These strange emotions are stirring up something inside of Red that he's been avoiding for years but now he seems ready to confront them.

It's a sunny day in Camden, a perfect day for a little shopping. Red isn't very social, and he certainly doesn't leave his home very often but today his mind is heavy on Fannie, and these thoughts of her is making him do things that he hasn't done in years. Red is slowly walking along the sidewalk on Grand Avenue where various shops and boutiques line both sides of the street.

※

Red casually enters Maggie's Gifts. There are a few customers browsing near the greeting cards and small stuff animals stands. Two ladies are looking at an abundant display of stylish earrings and necklaces along the left side near the front. Red heads toward the rear where he'd spotted an overhead 'Afro Centric' sign.

Red scans the small variety of greeting cards and few pieces of jewelry, mostly made of tiny colorful beads, in this small, tucked-away area. A lady wearing a puzzled expression approaches Red, "Can I help you with something?", she politely asks.

"Oh, I'm just looking for a little gift and maybe a nice card for a friend," Red nods.

"Sir, wouldn't you like to see our nicer merchandise upfront? We only put this back here because 'they' don't really come in here too much, but when they do come in we have to be politically correct nowadays because it don't take much to piss 'them' off, you know what I mean, don'tcha?", the lady says with a twisted face.

For a brief moment Red is frozen stiff. Facing this lady is as if he's actually facing his old self. Red doesn't normally share his inner feelings with no one but this moment is different and Red truly feels it.

Red looks the lady straight into her eyes and lets his heart speaks, "Ma'am, I lost my daughter because of that kind of thinking. I'm tired of hurting now. I ain't nobody to try to tell you how to live your life but maybe it's time to change your way of thinking. Like this little section back here, maybe it should be upfront."

As Mister Coles is in the midst of taking steps to change his life in Camden, the woman consuming his thoughts and desires is making her way towards Saint Louis along with the rest of the Lantern family.

Highway traffic is heavy as vehicles exit Interstate 70. Gracing the sky over St. Louis, the iconic Gateway Arch shines brightly in the midday sun.

The Lanterns' vivid RV exits the busy highway then makes its way towards the sizeable parking lot of Family Time Restaurant, where numerous TV satellite trucks from CNN, FOX, ABC, CBS and NBC have congregated along the northern side in anticipation of President Wheeler's scheduled arrival.

═══

On the southern side of the huge parking lot, a massive group of supporters are holding up handmade signs and banners reading 'Justice For Rico's Father', 'Bring Rico's Dad Back', 'Don't Deport Our American Soldiers', etc.

In the rear lot, near the restaurant green dumpsters, three shiny black Cadillac Escalades are parked a few spaces from Sherry's Mercedes-Benz.

The Lanterns' motley RV finds its way to the rear of the restaurant where orange safety cones are positioned and marked 'Reserved For America's Family'.

There's just as much activity going on inside the restaurant as there is outside. Behind closed doors in a spacious banquet room, shifty-eye Nick is fine-tuning details with President Wheeler as Misty stands by with all ears.

Nick briefs the President, "Dennis, all you gotta do to stay in compliance with the agreement is to simply say congratulations to the Lanterns for being America's Family on camera. That's it."

Misty chimes in, "Dennis, what exactly is this agreement?"

Startled, Nick rudely interjects as he gives Misty a look.

"Misty, did you just call him Dennis? Not just anybody can call him Dennis," Nick lectures.

Misty strikes back, "Mister President, I don't mean to disrespect you or your little boys club with Nick here and Mister Astor but today is quite different. It won't be me out there facing those cameras and all of those reporters. Today it's just you with the Lantern family. And you're going to have to spin your own bullshit, and if you want four more years in the White House then you better spin it good."

"Misty, I appreciate all of what you do and your concerns, but I think that I can handle this," President Wheeler nods assuringly.

Misty is doubtful of the President's somewhat cocky confidence, "Are you sure? Look, they're going to come at you hard out there. What's going to be your response when someone asks you about being paid for this appearance today?"

President Wheeler is stumped, as he looks at Nick for a save.

Misty interjects, "See, that's exactly what I'm talking about. You guys keep me out of the loop and then you fall flat on your fucking face and then you expect me to clean up your fucking shit."

Nick gives Misty a pompous smirk then adds, "Aww, it's true. Hm, 'Potty Mouth' Misty."

Misty sighs, realizing that it's useless trying to get through to these two.

───⊹⊱⊰⊹───

Meanwhile, back outside of the restaurant things are getting a bit testy. In the parking lot, the eclectic group of sign-toting supporters for Rico's dad has swollen into a chanting mob, led by a spirited group leader shouting, "Bring back Rico's dad!", in which the lively mob loudly repeats, "Bring back Rico's dad!"

An orange-tinged Dodge Ram pickup enters the parking lot. A Confederate flag is plastered over the pickup back window with 'Pro Gun', 'Wheeler For Wall' and 'Wheeler 4 More' bumper stickers ornamenting the shiny chrome. The orange Ram moves slowly through the lot, searching for an empty spot to park.

Behind the wheel of this slow-moving Ram sits a crusty, middle-age Southerner with a harden frown on his face as he gazes at the hordes of sign-toting folks filling the few empty parking spaces.

In the passenger seat the Southerner's wife rubs her stomach to ease her hunger.

"Don't look like we're gonna find a spot here, honey. Besides, I ain't particularly fond of being around these people anyway," the husband says while frowning at the mostly Black and Latina sign-toting crowd.

"Dang it, I wanted to try one of 'em new bean bowls too I keep hearing about," the wife sighs.

The gaudy pickup eases through the crowded lot, passing the ABC TV News crew prepping for a live broadcast near the parking lot exit.

In the background, the orange-tinged Ram leaves the lot as ABC News reporter Tony Downs and his skeletal crew goes live.

Tony looks directly into the camera, "Good afternoon. This is Tony Downs coming to you live from the gateway to the west, Saint Louis, Missouri. Although this is not an official campaign stop, national polls tell us that President Wheeler is struggling to connect with African-American and Hispanic voters, and, as you can see from this lively crowd in the parking lot here, President Wheeler's current immigration policy is certainly running into strong opposition."

The cameraman swerves the camera to give the TV audience a good view of the hordes of chanting supporters and their handmade banners and signs demanding, 'Justice For Rico's Dad', 'Bring Back Rico's Dad', etc.

Meanwhile, in the living room of the White House residential quarters, the President's daughter Emily, and her mother are curled up on the lengthy sofa in posh pajamas watching the tail end of Tony Down's news piece while sipping on afternoon coffee.

On the TV widescreen, the ABC News special report comes to an end, "From Saint Louis, this is Tony Downs keeping you informed. Thanks for watching."

Emily takes a sip of her coffee then looks at her mother. Seemingly, Emily wants to ask her mother something but only stares at her instead.

The First Lady notices her daughter awkwardly staring at her then nonchalantly asks, "Emily, are you sure you don't want some koloa in your coffee?"

Emily's not interested in her mom's question. Emily jumps into something much deeper.

"Mom, do you ever share your opinions with Dad about stuff in the news?", Emily asks.

"I used to, but now, well, I guess I'm just a silent partner."

"You're more than that, Mom. You're the First Lady, Mom. You have a real office just down the hallway from the Oval Office. You can do stuff, like real meaningful stuff."

"I know, honey. Dennis used to take me on his trips, like this one now in Saint Louis, but then I guess I just got in the way. I don't know."

"Whatcha think about what's going on now? I mean with Rico's father being deported to Mexico after he'd served years for America in the Air Force?"

There's a brief moment of silence as the First Lady absorbs her daughter's question, taking a long sip of her koloa-spiked coffee, then turns to Emily with a serious face.

"You know, Emily, men sometimes just want to fuck us then toss us aside like we're nothing. Rico's father put his life on the line for this country and now they just wanna fuck him. It's not right, not right at all," the First Lady utters with spirited conviction.

※

Genuinely surprised by her mother's sudden gumption, Emily smiles.

"Wow, Mom," Emily nods.

The First Lady springs up from the sofa then shakes her hair with a tease of newfound confidence.

"I think I'm gonna go to my office and get in touch with Homeland Security to get Rico's father back to where he truly belongs," the First Lady says.

A triumphant grin stretches across Emily's face.

"Hello," Emily cheers.

※

Back in St. Louis, in the main dining room of the bustling Family Time Restaurant, Secret Service agents are strategically positioned throughout the immense room.

Highway travelers from Interstate 70 and curious patrons are constantly turning their heads and glancing at the excitement in the center of the restaurant.

Camera clicks from the numerous photographers accentuate the noisy chatter throughout the dining room. TV cameras and the top news anchors from all of the major networks surrounds the lengthy table where President Wheeler is seated between dolled-up Terri and Grandma Fannie with Rico, Latoya, Ronnie, Darcy and Reggie filling in the rest of the chairs.

It's obvious that President Wheeler hates every moment of being here as he tries his best to conceal it behind an awkward, forced smile.

Taking full economical advantage of this national TV broadcast, bountiful dishes of all the popular Family Time menu specials, including the new Grandma Fannie's Bean Bowls, are on colorful display at the elongated table.

As two waitresses politely replenish everyone's drinks, President Wheeler slyly finger-push his serving of Grandma Fannie's Bean Bowl aside while giving an insincere nod to Grandma Fannie.

While nibbling on his fries, Ronnie is momentarily stunned when his roaming eyes catch the suited Secret Service agent posted near the side exit door.

Ronnie notices that the stern agent is one of the two agents who had confronted them earlier as they were nearing St. Louis on Interstate 70. Ronnie leans over to his sister Latoya and whispers something into her ear as she inconspicuously shifts her eyes toward the side exit door then gives a quick agreeable nod to Ronnie.

Standing within earshot to the left of the lengthy table, Nick and Misty looks on nervously as the President is about to face the national media alone.

Standing nearby to the right of the table, Sherry Will and the ever-delightful Meghan Whitman, who will be moderating this paramount press event today, are eagle-eyeing each and every move and detail.

Always camera-ready, Meghan glances at her watch then tactfully steps in between the line of TV cameras and the front of the table to make a quick announcement.

"The President is on a tight schedule. We have him for a few more minutes. We can squeeze in a couple questions," Meghan announces.

As Meghan steps out of the way, a CBS reporter fires a hard ball, "Mister President, you've been accused of accepting money for making appearances such as this one, and I'm sure you've already seen or possibly have read the series of articles in New York World by Brittany Stills that claims you're selling and profiting off of your presidency. Any response to that, Mister President?"

Only a few feet away, to the left of the President, Nick and Misty stand anxiously as they await President Wheeler's response.

Snake-tongue Nick has been schooling the President on the fine art of dodging bullets ever since he became the reelection campaign manager. This is a telling moment for the campaign if the proper response is well executed.

President Wheeler looks directly at the CBS reporter with a somewhat blank expression then utters an evasive answer, "Who is this Brittany Stills anyway? I bet she didn't even go to any type of accredited journalism school. If you want a real story, I would do a background check on this Miss Stills. Now there's your story right there."

This didn't go over well at all. Nick knows it, and Misty knows it. Nick shakes his head in disappointment as Misty silently mouths 'Fuck!'

The CBS reporter, along with every other news reporter and journalist in the crowded room, is taken aback, dumbfounded by President Wheeler's empty response.

Suddenly remembering his legal obligation to the signed agreement with Jake Astor, the President foolishly chooses this particular moment to congratulate the Lantern family.

"You know what, let's put all that negativity aside and celebrate the real reason why we're all here. What about winning that big nationwide contest, huh? Congratulations to Terrance Lantern and his family for being Family Time's 'America's Family!'", President Wheeler cheers wearing an apparent phony smile.

Continuing his act, the President claps halfheartedly as the dining room joins in, but the Lantern family will not hide their true feelings, regardless of all the national media attention. The obvious disdain for President Wheeler is evident as Rico purposely maneuvers his tattooed forearm to the cameras, and little Ronnie abruptly stands defiantly while looking squarely at the President, inadvertently raising quite a few eyebrows throughout the packed room.

The President puts on face as if he's actually interested while Ronnie speaks, "Um, Mister President, my name is Ronnie. I'm autistic. I read a lot and I remember stuff pretty good. I read those articles by Brittany Stills and I want you to know that she graduated from New York University with a master's degree in journalism and then she got her first job working for PBS and now she works at New York World. So, Mister President, Brittany Stills did go to a real journalism school."

Meanwhile, in New York City, Brittany is sitting on her lavish, white leather sofa comfortably close to her evening's date watching the special news report from St. Louis. Brittany's face melts as she watches eleven-year-old Ronnie defend her honor on national TV.

Brittany's date, Vince, has been trying to get serious with her for over four months, and unfortunately for him, he has picked a bad time to ask her, "So, are you going with anyone to the upcoming awards ceremony?"

While blushing as she watches young Ronnie on the TV screen, Brittany nods pleasingly, "Oh yes, I got my date, for sure."

Back in St. Louis, with every TV camera totally focused on him as he looks at President Wheeler, Ronnie has one more thing to get off of his chest, "And by the way, Mister President, you see that man right over there?"

Ronnie points to the suited Secret Service agent posted near the side exit door, then adds, "He tried to stop us from getting here to Saint Louis and I think he works for you."

The entire restaurant falls completely silent. Bewildered, President Wheeler looks to Nick and Misty to save him.

Nick sighs then hangs his head in defeat while Misty struggles to constrain her frustration. Seconds later, unable to suppress it any longer, Misty gives Nick a knowing 'I told you so' look, then unleashes a resounding 'Fuck!'

Reacting to Misty's predictable profaned outburst, two TV cameramen standing a few feet away, nod to one another with amused grins as one says, "Potty Mouth Misty. I swear, never fails."

―――

It's been a long day. The Lanterns are glad that the special media event with President Wheeler is over. In the Family Time Restaurant parking lot, as they each step up into the RV, Sherry is giving hugs and wishing each family member a safe trip on the last leg of their cross-country journey to Los Angeles.

Terri is the last one in line. Sherry looks at Terri admiringly then gently hooks her arm into his, gently guiding him a few steps away from the RV for a private conversation.

"Terri, can I ask you a question?", Sherry softly asks.

"What's up?", Terri nods.

"I'm curious. Why a lawyer, Terri?"

"You really wanna know?"

Sherry nods 'yes'.

⇌

Terri takes a deep breath as a past memory haunts him. Terri gathers himself as he prepares himself to recount the traumatic incident to Sherry that will change his life forever.

Sherry is all ears as Terri begins to speak, "A couple years ago, me, my friend Jay and a few others went to Cherry Hill. You know, the so-called good side of Camden. Two of us were turning sixteen so we thought that we'd go there to this real fancy ice cream parlor to kind of chill and celebrate. We sat down and waited for like maybe two or three minutes and then this manager, I guess, came out from the back somewhere and stood over us at our table with that certain look. You know, it's that kind of look that says that you don't belong here. I'll never forget that look. And then he said 'It's not Halloween yet so why are y'all dressed like that?' He wasn't looking for an answer 'cause right after he said that he straight up told us that he wasn't going to serve us anything."

Terri sighs as a lone tear streaks down his left cheek.

Holding back tears, Terri adds, "Ever since that day I would dream about becoming a lawyer to stop

America: No Purchase Necessary

shit like that. I never told my parents 'cause we just didn't have that kinda money for law school."

Sherry invitingly pulls Terri in for a tender hug then warmly offers, "Hey, while you guys are on the road to California maybe I'll make a few phone calls to some of my old college friends. There's one in particular who's deep into the legal field back east. I'll see if I can pull some strings for you Terri."

As the campaign season heats up, President Wheeler seems to be continually losing traction with minority voters across the country. It's been reported and well-documented that President Wheeler has a serious disconnect with people of color, and TV appearances by people in Washington, DC who have actually met the President is not helping the incumbent President at all on his poll numbers or with his reelection efforts, especially when popular politicians go on national TV and give anecdotal evidence of his indifference for certain populations.

In New York City, a live taping of the highly popular talk show 'Late Night with Sonny Connors' is already in progress. The studio audience sits attentively as the comedic host engages in a lively conversation with tonight's guest, Senator Bell.

"So, tell us, Senator Bell, as a young freshman Senator, are they treating you well in Washington?"

"For the most part they are, but of course there's always a few instances that makes you wanna scratch your head, especially when you introduce a new bill."

"Oh, that's right, you made the headlines when you helped write that bill about dress and hairstyle codes in public schools. Did you get a lot of support in Washington for that?"

"Support? Man, let me tell ya', I gotta real doozy here if you wanna hear it."

Coolly, Sonny turns to the studio audience and asks, "Y'all wanna hear it?"

The studio audience erupts with applause.

The young Senator dives into his story, "Well, President Wheeler didn't know who I was but he was kind enough to take a meeting with me. And get this, he must've thought that I was White because when one of the White House interns escorted me to the Oval Office, the President mistakenly took the intern, this young White guy, as me. And needless to say, that was a real awkward moment. But wait, there's more. Get this, during our little sit down, I started mentioning some of the different hairstyles that kids are wearing in school nowadays, like dreadlocks and corn rolls, and I kid you not, I think that I must've lost him at that point because once President Wheeler heard the term corn rolls, he sort of woke up and said 'A lot of people don't know this but there's a lot of Black farmers in America.' And wait, he didn't stop there. Believe it or not, this well-educated man, the President of this country went on to say that he saw a lot of corn rolls when he met some Black farmers during his campaign through Iowa."

The studio audience responds with laughter as Sonny adds, "So, the President wasn't really listening at all when you was trying to school him about the kids' different hairstyles."

"Not at all."

"Let me ask you this, Senator. Are you going to vote for another four more years for President Wheeler in November?"

"Sonny, I realize that this is a family show so please excuse my language, but hell no! Honestly, I just think that President Wheeler is so out of touch with everyday people. And, let me make this official right now on your show Sonny. Here tonight, I'm endorsing Senator April Taylor to be our next President of the United States!"

Sonny nods pleasingly, as the studio audience explodes with a rousing applause.

As he always does, President Wheeler likes to escape the campaign trail whenever he can and hobnob with the folks in his tight inner circle. At the prestigious Pine Hill Country Club in Fairfax, Virginia, a small group of Secret Service agents are standing guard on the lush green of the back nine, a short distance away from the President as he plays a round of golf with his largest campaign donor Jake Astor.

President Wheeler studies the trajectory of his next shot as Jake looks on with a pompous smirk then comments, "Dennis, are even here right now? You're doing it again. You're using a putter instead of a five iron on a shot like that."

"I don't know, Jake. It's that damn Lantern family. The fucking media keep putting out these stupid silly polls that says that people like them better than me! They think that they're so damn smart. Like they're more popular than me. Can you believe that? I'm the President. Nobody's more popular than me."

"Well, I don't mean to burst your little bubble there, Dennis, but actually, every time you're on TV your poll numbers drop, and to be quite honest with you, Family Time Restaurants is making a real killing on them new bean bowls, especially after every time America sees the Lanterns on TV."

President Wheeler sighs, then somewhat mindlessly switches clubs out of his golf bag propped up alongside their cart. Jake notices the President grabbing the wrong golf club but chooses not to say anything.

President Wheeler is feeling a distant tone from his golfing buddy today. He gives Jake a look then utters, "You seem to be enjoying this thing with the Lantern family, Jake. Hell, we've been friends a long time. Whose side are you on anyway?"

"Dennis, I've always been straight with you. I'm a business man, and a business man always loves the dollar, and to put it quite frankly, right now, it's the Lantern family who's making the dollar."

President Wheeler tightens his lips then releases his frustration with a hard swing at his golf ball.

The President eyes the ball as it takes flight then he slowly turns to Jake with the realization that his friendship with him has been based solely upon money.

Inadvertently, Jake rubs more salt into the President's wound, "As a matter of fact, Dennis, not too people have been coming to them big rowdy campaign rallies of yours lately, so being your main sponsor, we had to scale down your next rally in Richmond. Instead of the Richmond Coliseum, it's going to take place in Willy's backyard."

"Willy's backyard? What's that? Some kind of a catchy name for a big theater or what?"

"Actually, Dennis, it's literally Willy's backyard. He takes care of most of my RV dealerships along the Atlantic coast here and he's another golf buddy of mines. Ol' Willy's got one hell of a backyard. I swear, it stretches for miles, and besides that, he's all in, Dennis. He and his friends are die-hard Wheeler supporters. Hell, if it was up to Willy and his friends, your border wall would've been up and completely finished already. And just between you and me, Dennis, I think Willy and that close bunch that he hangs out with pretty much don't like anybody, if you know what I mean."

The President sighs, "So, you're telling me that my campaign rally went from a coliseum to a guy's backyard?"

Jake adds, "Hey, by the way, as your sponsor, I got all, if any, property damage covered, and all beers are already bought and paid for. Don't worry, Dennis, it'll be great. Oh, and plus too, I spoke with your campaign manager Nick and we're gonna make sure that everybody who shows up will get those catchy 'Wheeler for Wall' and them 'Wheeler 4 More' bumper stickers."

Right now, President Wheeler isn't paying attention to a single word out of Jake's out of mouth, as he struggles with the reality of the moment. Shaking his head in disbelief, the President utters, "A backyard?"

"Not just any ol' backyard, Willy's backyard," Jake nods.

Meanwhile, at the Mexican-American border, things are looking brighter for Rico's father as the First Lady's plan goes in motion.

On this clear sunny day in Laredo, Texas, the mighty Rio Grande flows calmly between America and Mexico. Separating the city of Laredo from its Mexican counterpart, Nuevo Laredo, is the bustling multi-lane Juaez Lincoln International Bridge. Every lane on the bridge is bumper-to-bumper with cars and trucks of all makes and sizes as uniformed inspectors and border guards diligently check each vehicle.

Across the majestic Rio Grande River, in Nuevo, Mexico, at a construction site, a crew of Hispanic workers is busy at work laying the foundation for a new apartment complex.

A white Border Patrol SUV, marked with a bold green stripe, rolls up to the construction site then parks alongside the workers' trucks.

Two uniformed border patrol officers and professionally-dressed Homeland Security representative Christina May step out of the green-striped SUV then make their way towards the hustling construction workers as they pour concrete and carefully set cinder blocks.

Christina is carrying a sealed envelope in her right hand as they near the crew. The workers momentarily stop as Christina and the two officers approaches.

In a thick Spanish accent, Christina greets the crew, "Where's the beer? No cerveza? Com'on, we can't work like this without cerveza."

Amused, everyone cracks a smile as Christina continues, "Hola, is there a Eduardo Garcia here?"

Thirty-five-year-old Eduardo Garcia wipes the beads of sweat from his forehead with the back of his hand then steps forward, "I'm Ed," he says.

"Mister Garcia, your family told us where to find you," Christina acknowledges then hands the sealed envelope to Eduardo.

Mister Garcia accepts the envelope with a baffled expression as Christina goes on to elaborate, "First of all, on behalf of the American people, thank you for your service in the United States Air Force. And, in that envelope, you will find your certified American citizenship papers, new ID, and from the Forst Lady herself, a check to cover your travel and housing set up back in the U.S."

Excitedly, Eduardo opens the envelope and quickly thumbs through the contents as his fellow coworkers stand proudly and begin to applaud him. Christina and the two patrol officers join the applause as Eduardo looks skyward and mouths 'Thank you, God.'

My grandma said that when she was little back in South Carolina they used to go to church all the time but when she came to New Jersey then they didn't go too much 'cause she said that sometimes you can already be in church and be sitting right at home at the same time. Just like a lot of stuff my grandma tells me I didn't understand what she meant at first, but now I do though. It's like what the First Lady did for Rico's father. My grandma says that she don't know for sure if you're gonna go to heaven when you do something good for somebody else, but she says that, at least, you're gonna get your foot in heaven's door. And I think that what the President's wife did for Mister Garcia is probably the best gift anybody can give to somebody else, and I'm pretty sure she gotta good chance of getting in 'heaven.

As blessings are bestowed upon Rico's father across the border, the Lanterns' colorful RV shines in the Kansas sun while cruising westward. Picturesque, bountiful fields of lofty sunflowers flank the desolate Interstate 70 highway cutting through this long stretch of rural Kansas.

Behind the wheel, Reggie is in awe of the abundant beauty of the vibrant sunflower fields.

Equally amazed, Darcy looks out the passenger side window in a mesmerizing daze at the stunning sunflowers.

Reggie is overwhelmed by the beauty on both sides of the highway, "I tell ya', Darcy, this is something special right here. I swear, you can't even put a price on where we're at."

Darcy nods agreeably, "You're so right, babe. Hm, just look at us now. You can't buy stuff like this. Hm, and to think that we got all of this from Terri filling out a simple survey. Hm, no purchase necessary."

As the RV makes its way through Kansas, a little further down the hallway, Rico steps out of the restroom then casually walks back to the room he shares with Latoya.

With his hand on the door handle, Rico abruptly freezes as he hears Latoya's voice apparently speaking to someone on the phone.

While standing outside the closed door, Rico faintly hears Latoya saying, "I can't wait to see you in L.A."

Rico is crushed. He can't believe he'd just heard those words come out of girlfriend's mouth.

Devastated, Rico walks away and retreats to the kitchenette further down the hallway.

In the kitchenette, Grandma Fannie is stirring one of her spicy bean dishes atop the customized, no-slip range as young Ronnie quietly reads one of his magazines at the table.

Rico enters and instantly deflates at the small table, resting his head into his open palms.

Grandma Fannie turns around and concernly asks, "Rico? Is everything okay, baby?"

⇌

With his head still resting in his palms atop the table, Rico doesn't respond to Grandma Fannie.

Concerned, Grandma Fannie lightly taps Ronnie's shoulder, "Ronnie, will you go get your mama, please?"

Ronnie springs up and immediately heads toward the front of the RV.

A minute later, Darcy enters the kitchenette and takes a seat across from Rico as Grandma Fannie turns off the range then points to Rico with a baffled expression.

"Rico, did something happened between you and Latoya?", Darcy asks.

His head still buried in his palms, Rico seems lost as he blankly looks down at the table, never making eye contact with Darcy or Grandma Fannie.

Darcy shrugs her shoulders at Grandma Fannie, then abruptly, Rico softly utters, "I think Latoya's messing around with somebody."

"What makes you say that, Rico?", Darcy asks.

"When I came back from the bathroom, I heard her talking on the phone to some dude."

Grandma Fannie chimes in, "What exactly did she say, Rico?"

"I didn't hear everything but she did say something about meeting him L.A."

Unbeknownst to Rico, everyone else is aware of his father's new citizenship and they've been secretly planning a surprise celebration when they arrive in Los Angeles. Darcy and Grandma Fannie are always up for a little fun so Rico just provided them with the perfect opportunity. Immediately, like two playful school girls, Darcy and Grandma Fannie glance at one another with knowing grins and then Darcy gives her mother-in-law a nod and a wink.

Putting on her best sincere face, Darcy scoots closer to Rico while Grandma Fannie tries her hardest to contain her laughter bubbling inside her stomach.

"Rico, look at me, talk to me. What were the exact words you heard Latoya say?", Darcy asks while inconspicuously winking again at Grandma Fannie.

Slowly, Rico looks directly at Darcy. Grandma Fannie puts her hands over her stomach then turns away to prevent herself from exploding with laughter.

Rico sighs, then struggles to repeat what he heard Latoya say, "I'm not one hundred percent sure, but I think she said 'I can't wait to see you in L.A.'"

Grandma Fannie turns around and is near eruption as Darcy continues her farce.

"I knew it. My daughter's a skank," Darcy jokes while struggling to keep a straight face.

Once again, Darcy sneaks a quick wink at her mother-in-law, this time signaling her to join in.

Grandma Fannie easily reads Darcy's wink and immediately adds to the farce, "Yeah Rico, I knew Latoya was a skank too."

Abruptly, Latoya appears at the kitchen entrance. She's puzzled to see Rico sitting at the table looking distraught.

"What's going on? Rico, you said that you was going to the bathroom," Latoya asks.

Before Rico gets a chance to respond, Darcy quickly interjects, "Well Latoya, um, after Rico told me and your grandmother about this particular phone conversation he'd overheard a little while ago, well, me and your grandmother here was kind of discussing the likelihood that you might be a skank."

Taken aback, Latoya utters, "A what?"

Trying her best to maintain a straight face, Darcy continues her farce, "A skank."

Unable to contain it any longer, Grandma Fannie erupts and double over with laughter as Darcy quickly join in with uncontrollable giggling.

At that moment, it hits Latoya, as she realizes that Rico must've overheard her talking to his father.

Latoya sighs as she tries to explain, "Rico, that was your father on the phone. He wanted to surprise you in L.A."

Latoya shoots her giggling mother and grandmother a scolding look then adds, "We were supposed to keep the news about your father a secret but I guess some people just can't help themselves."

Rico turns to Darcy and Grandma Fannie, "You two knew all along?"

Darcy is having too much fun with this. She can't seem to stop herself as she inconspicuously winks at Grandma Fannie while speaking to Rico, "Com'on now, Rico, let's put this puzzle together. Think about it. A pretty girl like Latoya. And remember those exact words you heard 'I can't wait to see you in L.A.' Hm, sounds like one of them hookups. Hm."

Once again, just like two giddy school girls, Darcy and Grandma Fannie burst into laughter as Latoya sighs, "Com'on, Rico. Let's go. Terri was right. These people are crazy. Plain crazy."

Meanwhile, in Washington, in the White House press briefing room, all eyes and TV cameras are focused on Misty as she stands alone behind the podium delivering the President's latest developments and spinning the President's missteps to the eager press corps, "And this administration is committed to strong bipartisanship, regardless of what side of the aisle the bill originated from. President Wheeler wants a strong America, and if that means keeping some people out then so be it."

Misty glances at her watch as a few antsy journalists and reporters position their hands to shoot up. Misty gives them their cue, "Okay, just a few questions."

Instantly, several hands sprout up throughout the room. Misty points to the CNN reporter seated in the middle of the room.

"Misty, maybe you can clear something up here. On one hand, I'm getting the message that this administration is firm on certain immigration policies and tighter border control issues, but yet, Mister Garcia, as I'm sure you already know, is the Air Force veteran who was deported back to Mexico, and is now returning to the states. What transpired to cause this flip?"

Misty is completely caught off-guard by the reporter's question. She's baffled, awkwardly dumbfounded.

Misty looks squarely at the CNN reporter then clearly asks, "I'm sorry, did you say that Mister Garcia is now returning to the states?"

"Yes," the reporter quickly nods.

Misty is still confused but tries to save face with a half-hearted response, "Well, if Mister Garcia crosses the border illegally then he'll be caught and processed to be deported again just like all of the others who cross illegally."

The CNN reporter waves his hand to speak again as he realizes that Misty possibly may not have a clue on these recent developments, "No, no. Maybe you misunderstood, Misty. This administration. This White House just recently, just officially reversed Mister Garcia's immigration status, and now Mister Garcia has full citizenship status just like you and I. Were you not aware of this, Misty?"

Misty has been left out of the loop numerous times before by the President himself, and especially by the President's sneaky campaign manager Nick, that it's now reaching a boiling point. Misty sighs as the entire press corps looks on. Misty doesn't answer the CNN reporter's question. Strangely, Misty stands at the podium wearing a blank expression for a few long seconds, then abruptly, she hastily throws her arms up in the air while storming away towards the side door!

America: No Purchase Necessary

Misty is clearly pissed off as the entire press room loudly hears Misty's "Fuck!" just before she vanishes out the side door.

Along the right side of the press room, a TV cameraman digs out a five-dollar bill from his wallet then hands it to another TV cameraman standing nearby, "You was right, Bob. Potty Mouth Misty strikes again."

⇒≑⇐

Meanwhile, in the Oval Office, trademarked red, white and blue carry-out bags from Family Time Burgers rest atop the furniture as Nick and a small entourage of White House staffers and interns huddle around President Wheeler's desk. They're all looking at and discussing something atop the desk apparently of great importance. While nibbling on fries and taking little spoonfuls from their Grandma Fannie's bean bowls, everyone's twisted facial expressions reveal something displeasing atop the desk.

Although no one is watching, along the wall, the five widescreen TV monitors are on and showing Misty in slow motion as she throws her arms up in frustration, stepping away from the podium then letting loose her distinctive, profaned 'Fuck!' while a flashing news ticker slowly crawls across the bottom of each network's screen, informing 'WHITE

HOUSE PRESS SECRETARY 'POTTY MOUTH' MISTY DOES IT AGAIN!'

Suddenly, Misty bursts through the door! Misty is pissed!

"Why didn't someone tell me about Mister Garcia?", Misty loudly scorns.

Everyone huddled around the President's desk pops their head up with puzzled faces.

"Mister Garcia?", President Wheeler asks while turning to Nick.

"The Mexican kid's father," Nick replies.

Misty is furious. Angrily, she hits back, "Don't play fucking dumb with me! You know exactly who I'm talking about."

And to everyone's surprise, the door swings open again. This time, all heads immediately turn as the First Lady and her daughter Emily strolls in with a bit of attitude and sass.

President Wheeler's mouth drops as he stares at his wife's stylish dress and gorgeous hair, something he hasn't seen on her for quite a while.

With all eyes glued on her, the First Lady steps in front of Misty and coolly utters, "Misty, I saw your press briefing. Um, I think I made a boo boo. You see, I didn't quite agree with how Mister Garcia was being treated, so, thanks to a big push from my lovely daughter here I just thought that I would use my influence as First Lady to make things right. But

I made a boo boo 'cause I forgot to send you the memo."

Sitting quietly at his desk, President Wheeler softly whispers to Nick, "Can she do that?"

Nick shrugs his shoulders. The First Lady gives her husband and Nick a look, letting them both know that she'd read them well.

Emily checks the time on her cellphone then alerts the First Lady, "Mom. The driver."

The First Lady turns directly to her husband and says, "Yes, Dennis, I can do that. And I see the usual fries and all, but would you like to join me and Emily for lunch at this new French place on Fourteenth?"

⇒++⇐

President Wheeler inconspicuously glances at the Japanese characters tattooed on Emily's forearm then makes his decision, "No honey, I'm good. You and Emily go and enjoy yourselves. We have a situation here."

"Hm, I kind of figured that," the First Lady says with a knowing nod.

The First Lady steps toward the door to leave as Emily looks back at her dad with disappointment in her eyes then joins her mother out the door.

Nick turns to Misty, "We actually do have a situation here, Misty. Come look at this."

Misty walks over to the desk as President Wheeler holds up the glossy magazine cover of the latest print edition of New York World, depicting a colorful photo of President Wheeler donning a forced smile while seated between dolled-up Terri and Grandma Fannie at the big media event in St. Louis. In the glossy picture, neither Terri or Grandma Fannie looks happy to be there. The magazine cover caption reads 'America's Family Gives President Cold Shoulders.'

"Of all the families in America why in the hell 'this family got picked for America's Family? The Lanterns ain't America. I'm America! They've been nothing but a headache," President Wheeler sighs.

"More like a migraine. The money and campaign donations sure ain't coming in like it used to. Lord knows what's going to happen once this cover hits the public," Nick adds.

"No more arenas and stadiums. I guess I have to get use to peoples' backyards," the President says while struggling to accept his current reality.

Misty takes a deep breath then begins to rip into the President and his sheisty campaign manager, "Guys, if you fucking want to turn things around and get your base pumped up again you need to get fucking serious and stop stepping in your own shit! You better prepare for this upcoming debate in San Diego 'cause if you don't then we're all going to be out of a fucking job. Hell, this magazine cover is nothing compared to the hard shit Senator Taylor's gonna throw at you in San Diego, so if you really want four more years you can't afford to drop the fucking ball this time."

Nick moans with a condescending then takes a shot at the boisterous press secretary, "Misty, I'm not one to be judgy but your mouth really is kind of potty."

⇌⇋

CHAPTER 9
APRIL RISING

Home to the world-famous San Diego Zoo and the majestic Coronado Bridge that graces over the San Diego Bay, this coastal city will have everyone's attention this evening as it hosts the first televised Presidential debate of the campaign season.

On the stage at the San Diego Convention Center, standing straight in perfect posture, presidential candidate Senator April Taylor is behind the podium to the left of incumbent President Dennis Wheeler.

The two eager candidates are facing a table of three moderators, TV cameras, and an attentive audience of college students, local professionals and selected guests.

One of the moderators gets things started as she looks directly at the popular Senator, "Senator Taylor, this question is for you. Particularly, in the last year, you've seen how President Wheeler has conducted himself. Hypothetically, if you were the current President, would you had done anything differently?"

⇌

"I certainly wouldn't try to sell or wouldn't try to make a profit from making appearances as certain celebrities do. I think that what we saw in St. Louis recently is the actions of a pimp," Senator Taylor bluntly states.

"Pimp? Are you calling me a whore? What are you saying?", President Wheeler interjects.

The three moderators glance at one another with amused grins.

"What I'm saying is that you were paid for your appearance in St. Louis, and I mean paid with a capital 'p' by your golfing buddy, who also happens to be the owner and CEO of the Family Time Corporation," Senator Taylor quickly answers.

President Wheeler wants to respond but seems to be struggling to find the right words. He stands embarrassed with a tighten lip.

One of the moderators asks, "Mister President, would you like to respond to Senator Taylor's remarks?"

There's an awkward moment of silence as President Wheeler's face grows angry then begins to point directly at the table of moderators. The President begins to scold the three moderators, "Why should I respond to made up lies and allegations? If you people did your job you would've stopped her from airing this phony hog wash."

Calmly, one of the moderators asks, "Mister President, is it true that you were paid to participate in the 'America's Family' Sweepstakes event in St. Louis with the Lantern family?"

The President looks disoriented, as if he's been hit by a bomb. He doesn't know how to respond, then abruptly he hits back with, "What a rotten question. How'd you get picked as a moderator?"

Senator Taylor has heard enough. She turns to President Wheeler with fire in her eyes and lets loose something that she's been dying to say all evening, "Mister President, with all due respect, you are the President of the United States! And that office, sir, is NOT for sale!"

Meanwhile, in Frederick, Maryland, comfortably snuggled on their cozy couch in the living room, Misty Madsen and her husband are watching the Presidential debate in San Diego on their Sony widescreen. Misty turns to her husband, "Honey, are they hiring at your company? I'm gonna be out of a job 'cause we're about to get our first female president."

Back in San Diego, the televised debate is near the end as the moderators begin to thank the President and Senator April Taylor for attending, "Senator Taylor and Mister President, on behalf of the City of

San Diego, we would like to thank you both for a very informative and lively debate."

⇌

President Wheeler and Senator Taylor politely nod 'thank you', as one of the moderators adds, "And good luck to you both as you continue on the campaign trail. Senator Taylor, I believe you have a huge town hall event in Denver next week so we wish you well on that, and Mister President I understand that you have a rally coming up next week as well at the Richmond Coliseum in Virginia so ---"

The speaking moderator is momentarily interrupted as one of his colleagues leans over and whisper something into his ear. A few seconds later, the speaking moderator makes a correction, "I'm sorry. Correction, Mister President, um, we wish you well in Richmond at um, Willy's backyard."

⇌

CHAPTER 10
LATOYA'S DILEMMA

Traveling westward along Highway 64 near the South Rim of the Grand Canyon National Park, the bright Arizona sun illuminates the vibrant rainbow colors layered throughout the mile-deep canyon.

The Lanterns' RV is making its way along the curvy highway towards the spacious parking area adjacent to the South Rim's Overlook.

A few minutes later, standing side by side along the railing of the overlook, Reggie, Darcy, Grandma Fannie, Latoya, Ronnie, Rico, and Terri are all awestruck by the majestic view and splendor of the beautiful canyon. They stand speechless, slowly taking in such a magnificent view of America that they've never imagined.

In the parking area, a family of five exits their van then excitedly starts pointing at the embolden words alongside the flag-colored RV parked nearby, spelling 'America's Family Sweepstakes Winner'. Eagerly, the family of five looks around and quickly spot the Lanterns standing side by side along the overlook railing.

Hastily pulling out their cellphones, the family of five rush over to the Lanterns and politely request to take selfies with them. Somewhat surprised by the request, the Lanterns blush briefly, then Terri begins to show off his many poses, striking one dramatic pose after another with each selfie taken.

Seemingly out of nowhere, a young couple approaches the Lantern family with their cellphones in hand and politely requesting a selfie. Once again, collectively, the Lanterns blush at their notoriety then happily pose with the grateful couple.

About an hour later, while the rest of the family are having their lunch inside the bustling Market Plaza at the huge Grand Canyon Visitor Center along with hordes of other travelers and tourists, Latoya and Terri are outside in the picnic area having their lunch alone at a redwood table topped with a wide umbrella.

Latoya's plate consists of two orders of fried onion rings and one order of fries. Terri takes a bite of his burger as Latoya sips her Pepsi. While slowly chewing his burger, Terri teases his sister, "Latoya, can you tell me the four food groups we all learned about in school?"

"I know, I know. What can I say, I just love me some rings and fries, that's all."

"So, you don't know."

"I do know."

"Well?"

"Bread, milk, vegetables and meat. Satisfied?"

Amused, Terri smiles then his face turns serious as he looks directly at Latoya and asks, "Hey sis', so why did you wanted to talk to me?"

"It's Rico. I mean, you and the whole family knows that we're not doing anything but I can tell that Rico is starting to want more, you know."

"Did he ask you?"

"No, he didn't say anything but I can just tell, kind of sense it."

"If he seriously came at you like that, how would you react?"

"Honestly, Terri, I don't know. I do love Rico and we kid around a lot n' stuff, but 'that', I really don't know."

"I'm about to throw something at you right now but it's gonna cost you. For what I'm about to lay on you should be about four onion rings," Terri nods.

Latoya smiles as she places three onion rings on Terri's plate.

"Oh, I see, you think I'm playing."

Amused, Latoya places another fried onion ring on Terri's plate.

Terri begins to lay some wisdom on his little sister, "You know, sis', you and Rico have been friends ever since, what, like third grade and on top of that, Rico's like family to us all, especially after we took him in after his dad's situation. And sis', that maybe the problem right there. Me, Ronnie, everybody, we all kind of look at Rico like family, and maybe you do too. If you ain't feeling it like in 'that way' then Rico's become your brother."

Latoya ponders deeply, slowly absorbing the thought, as Terri nonchalantly eats his onion rings.

Latoya begins to stare at Terri as he devours his food. Quietly, she nods pleasingly as she humbly appreciates his insight. Thanking him, Latoya tosses two more fried onion rings onto Terri's plate.

"Girl, I love you too. You know you're my favorite sister, right?"

"I'm your only sister."

"You don't know that. Who knows what Dad's been doing."

"Terri, you're just too much," Latoya says while looking at her older brother with nothing but pure love in her eyes.

CHAPTER 11
HOLLYWOOD

Traveling on the crammed California Highway 101, the Lanterns' luxury RV is in the flow of traffic cutting through Los Angeles, the entertainment capital and true mecca for every musician and actor everywhere.

Latoya is awestruck as she looks out the window at the place she's been dreaming about for most of her life.

The eye-catching, 45-foot-high Hollywood sign ornament the south side of the Hollywood Hills. The lofty Capitol Records Tower sits near the famous intersection of Hollywood and Vine, where the star-studded Hollywood Walk of Fame highlights the sidewalks along Hollywood Boulevard.

The Lanterns' flag-themed RV exits Highway 101 then merges onto Sunset Boulevard towards the Sunset Television Studios.

America: No Purchase Necessary

About an hour later, in one of the elaborate green rooms at the Sunset Television Studios, the Lanterns are gathered together before they make their very first talk show appearance on the popular 'Your America' program. Terri, Ronnie, and Rico are nibbling at an assortment of appetizing finger foods displayed atop a lengthy table running along the right side.

Above the table spread of finger snacks, large golden letters spell out 'THIS IS YOUR AMERICA' along the wall.

Sitting on a plush couch, Reggie and Darcy are sipping on tea while anxiously anticipating the family's cue to go on stage.

In the left corner, Sherry is briefing Latoya and Grandma Fannie about their TV commercial shoot, "They're over there now setting up, so right after this taping we need to head directly there. I already gave Reggie the address on Santa Monica Boulevard," Sherry nods while turning towards Rico, "And Rico, by the way, I've made arrangements for your dad to be picked up at LAX so he'll meet you at the restaurant."

The door swings. A cheerful production assistant enters and announces, "Is everybody ready? We're about to get called on set."

As the young production assistant holds the door open with her back, the host can be heard making his introduction of the Lanterns, "You're in for a real big treat now, folks. On a show where we showcase the positive lives of everyday people and remind folks that this is your America too, how lucky are we to have, on this very stage today, 'America's Family', the wonderful Lantern family from Camden, New Jersey!"

From the green room, the Lanterns can loudly hear the studio audience giving a rousing applause.

The spirited production assistant motions the family to follow her as she escorts them onto the stage. One by one, Rico and the Lanterns step out into the hallway, leaving Sherry alone in the green room.

Sherry's cellphone rings. Sherry answers, "Hello... Oh, hey! Finally. Hey, I've been trying to reach you. I got this really great kid who wants to go into the legal field and I was hoping to connect you two....Sure. He'll be back in Jersey in a couple weeks and I'll text you all the details...Thanks, bye."

⊨╬⊨

Forty minutes later, on the stage sitting comfortably on two elongated couches, the Lanterns are enjoying their notoriety as the host brings the live taping to a close in front of the enthusiastic studio audience, "I gotta be honest with you, I meet a lot of people day in and day out, especially with a job like mines, but trust me when I say this. These seven individuals here up on this stage with me right now are the most genuine and everyday people I've ever met."

The studio audience readily agrees and explodes with applause.

The host turns and looks directly at the Lanterns, sitting side by side on the two lengthy couches, and invitingly asks, "Now, before we say goodbye, is there anything either one of you would like to share with our audience here and folks in TV land?"

The Lanterns all glance at one another then Darcy nods pleasingly, gesturing that she'll be happy to say something.

The host politely gives Darcy his 'go ahead' nod.

Darcy waves to the attentive audience then humbly begins to speak, "You know, it's true that there's a lot of ugly stuff going on in America right now, but I just wanna say that just like a lot of y'all we never had a lot of money to travel outside of Camden and really go anywhere, but I gotta tell ya', on this trip, we've seen how beautiful this country really is. Y'all should've seen all of them beautiful sunflowers when we was going through Kansas. I wanted to tell Reggie to stop so I could go out and cut a few of them down but I didn't wanna get arrested so I just kept that to myself."

The studio audience erupts with laughter, loving every moment of Darcy's story.

On cue, the host brings the show to a close, "Thank you, Darcy. And maybe, folks, we can all take a lesson from that and try to get out more, if we can, and try to see the beauty in this great country of ours. And on that note, it's been a pleasure and always remember that this is your America too."

―――

A couple hours later, at Family Time Burgers on Santa Monica Boulevard, a film production crew has taken over half of the dining area and is prepping for a commercial shoot along the right side.

Sound, lighting, and camera equipment are scattered everywhere as certain booths are being dressed with perfectly-placed ketchup and mustard bottles, napkin holders, and salt and pepper shakers by a finicky set designer.

―――

Along the rear wall, a group of actors dressed as police officers and firefighters are adjusting their uniforms.

Attired in a waitress skirt, Latoya is in pure heaven, enjoying every second of this moment as an aging makeup artist touches up her face in the far-right corner.

At a nearby table, Grandma Fannie is going over her line with the script supervisor. Grandma Fannie is reading word-for-word directly from the script in her hands, "Don't tell anybody but Family Time makes my bean bowls better than I do."

Grandma Fannie looks at the script supervisor with a disapproving frown.

The script supervisor is puzzled by Grandma Fannie's frown, "What's wrong? You read that perfectly, Fannie."

"So, you want me to lie? Ain't nobody making my bean bowls better than me. Ain't no way."

"I understand, Fannie, but this is just a TV commercial, a sales pitch. We're just simply trying to get people to come to Family Time to get your bean bowls, that's all."

Grandma Fannie sighs.

The script supervisor adds, "And, one more thing, Fannie, when you're interacting with the waitress, can you say your line with a bit more conviction, like you really mean it?"

Grandma Fannie begins to smile then nods, "Oh, trust me, honey. I'm always gonna speak my mind."

Nearby, a production assistant is placing a variety of Grandma Fannie Bean Bowls atop a waitress cart near one of the immaculate booths prepped with the properly-placed condiment bottles.

Terri, Ronnie, Darcy, Reggie, Rico and his father Eduardo are standing a few steps behind the film crew, proudly observing Latoya and Grandma Fannie get made up for their big acting debut.

Reggie is looking directly at Latoya. Reggie assumes he'd made eye contact with his daughter so he excitedly waves to her. There's no response from Latoya as the wardrobe stylist adjusts her waitress uniform.

⇌

Darcy turns to Reggie and jokes, "Don't worry 'bout it, babe. You know how them Hollywood types are. I swear, as soon as they get a little fame then they don't know you."

Reggie cracks a smile at his wife's playfulness.

Terri is looking directly at Grandma Fannie as she sits alone at one of the booths. Terri begins to smile as he observes his grandmother sneakily retrieves a political campaign button from her purse then inconspicuously tries to pin it on her blouse.

Terri taps his parents' shoulders then whispers, "Y'all see what Grandma's doing?"

Reggie and Darcy begin to giggle lightly as they watch Grandma Fannie trying to pin the colorful campaign button on her blouse.

As Grandma Fannie brings the 'Senator April Taylor For President' campaign button up to her lapel, seemingly out of nowhere, the finicky set designer coolly slides into the booth then scoots close to her.

Grandma Fannie attempts to hastily stuff the campaign button back into her purse but the set designer surprisingly shakes his head 'no' then calmly utters, "Fannie, I've been doing this a long time. Hardly anything gets pass me. When I saw how you wanted to show your love for April Taylor, well, I said that I could either go over there and yell at her for wearing something that was political in nature, which, by the way, is a big 'no no' in these types of commercials, or I could go over there and tell this nice lady how much I absolutely despise President Wheeler and his heartless ass, and give her a better-looking button to put on her nice blouse."

Coolly, the set designer retrieves a more vibrant 'Senator April Taylor For President' campaign button from his shirt pocket then leans over to pin it on Grandma Fannie's lapel.

The set designer slips out from the booth as Grandma Fannie smiles triumphantly.

Standing out of the way, behind two lighting screens, Sherry is talking to Meghan Whitman, the always-perky spokesperson for the Family Time Corporation. Meghan nods pleasingly while discussing the overall success of the national Family Time sweepstakes with Sherry.

Agreeing with Meghan, Sherry adds, "From all the media coverage it looks like President Wheeler didn't exactly get the outcome that he'd wanted from this whole ordeal, but Family Time couldn't have asked for anything better."

Meghan nods, "That's putting it mildly, Sherry. This has been a homerun for us. With the help of the Lanterns, our sales have quadrupled compared to last quarter, and it's steadily rising."

The nit-picking set designer is inspecting the set. He abruptly stops and begins to look at one of the booths sideways, awkwardly twisting his head and neck while doing so. He doesn't like what he sees and loudly berates, "Who moved the ketchup? Everybody knows that the ketchup goes on the right and the mustard goes on the left!"

Lighthearted giggling spreads throughout the crew as the jaded makeup artist puts the finishing touches on Latoya, "Hollywood sure got some real characters. Honey, are you sure you really want this Hollywood life?", she asks Latoya.

Without any hesitation whatsoever, Latoya nods, "More than anything."

The energetic director steps to the center of the set to get everyone's attention and announces, "Okay people, be ready in three for our first run-through."

Everyone scatters. Actors take their places. All props are properly positioned. Sound, lighting, and camera people are all in place.

All eyes and cameras are on the three booths along the right side. The first booth has two police officers with a two-way radio centered atop the table. The second booth consists of four firefighters and a two-way radio atop their table as well. At the third booth, Grandma Fannie sits alone, looking content as she waits for the waitress.

Down the aisle, near the first booth, attired in her waitress outfit, Latoya stands next to the waitress cart stacked with a wide assortment of GRANDMA FANNIE'S BEAN BOWLS. Latoya is awaiting her cue to start.

Seconds later, the director instructs, "Quiet on the set and action!"

Always camera-ready, perky Family Time spokesperson Meghan Whitman steps in front of the cameras and perfectly delivers her pitch, "Here at Family Time we serve a wide variety of menu items, but sometimes our customers just want one thing."

As Meghan steps aside the director signals Latoya to start. On cue, Latoya rolls her cart next to the booth of police officers and puts on her big, cheerful waitress smile, "Hi, welcome to Family Time. May I take your order, please?"

A red light begins to blink on the two-way radio atop the table. From the speaker on the blinking two-way, a loud voice is heard from police dispatch, "Unit Five, we have a ten-sixty-five in progress at Pacific Bank, that's seven-one-twelve Santa Monica."

Nonchalantly, the police officers look at Latoya to take their order. Latoya, on the other hand, puts on her best puzzled face and delivers her lines, "But aren't you gonna take care of that? Isn't that a bank robbery?"

One of the police officers casually says, "Oh somebody'll get that. We both will have your Ranch Bean Bowls."

Latoya hands the officers two Ranch bowls from her cart then steps toward the next booth seated with the four firefighters. Again, Latoya puts on her wide waitress smile, "Hi, welcome to Family Time. May I take your order, please?"

On cue, the red light starts blinking on the firefighters' two-way radio. A loud voice from their station dispatch alerts, "Ladder Nine, we have a house fire at eight-six-ten Venice."

Latoya notices how either of the four firefighters are eager to spring up and respond to the call. Latoya dramatically sighs, "Let me guess. Somebody'll get that."

Right on cue, one of the firefighters casually nods, "Certainly. Now can we get two of your Spicy

Cinnamon Bean Bowls and two of your Butter Cream Bowls?"

Politely, Latoya hands the four bowls to the firefighters, then moves to her third and final booth.

Grandma Fannie knows that her booth is next. Slyly, she shifts her body so that the cameras can get a better shot of her 'Senator April Taylor For President' campaign button on her lapel.

Latoya approaches the booth with a big, convincing Hollywood smile, "Hi, welcome to ---- Oh, it's you!"

Latoya holds up one of the containers from her waitress cart then compares the likeness of Grandma Fannie's face colorfully displayed on the plastic container to the lady sitting in the booth.

Putting her best acting skills to work, Latoya's eyes widen with surprise as she excitedly says, "It is you! You're Grandma Fannie! Whatcha doin' here?"

"Don't tell anybody but Family Time makes my bean bowls better than I do. Hm, like that's true," Grandma Fannie says with a bit of a sneer.

"Cut!," the director angrily yells while eyeing the script supervisor.

Sighing, the script supervisor looks directly at Grandma Fannie who is simultaneously giving a wink and a nod to the script supervisor.

The director moans then motion the script supervisor to come closer for a chat.

"I warned her not to," the script supervisor readily admits.

Disappointedly shaking his head, the director sighs, "We can always edit."

⇌

Meanwhile, back in Washington at the White House, the President's free-spirited daughter Emily and her Nigerian-born friend Deon are walking along the corridor near the Oval Office. A White House security guard casually strolls by the young couple with an obvious eye on Deon.

Walking closely beside Emily, Deon abruptly stops as they stand next to the Oval Office door. Deon's face turns curious then asks, "You hear that?"

Emily eases her left ear closer to the door. Emily hears her mother's harden voice as she unleashes on her husband, "I can't believe you would even ask me that, Dennis! You want me to go on national TV and say that I had a lapse in judgement? I did what I did for Mister Garcia because it was the right thing to do! Look Dennis, your poll numbers ain't dropping because of me. They're low because of all the shit you and Nick have been piling up! Only you can save you, Dennis, not me!"

Suddenly, the door opens.

Stepping out into the corridor with a touch of brashness and cool, the First Lady is immediately face to face with her daughter, as Emily nods her head admiringly, "Way to go, Mom."

⇌

Emily high-fives her mother, then the First Lady looks at Deon with genuine sincerity in her eyes, "Hey Deon, make sure you stop by my office before you leave today. I got a little something for you," she says.

"I will," Deon nods.

The First Lady strolls away with confidence in her step as Deon follows Emily into her father's office.

The Oval Office is solemnly quiet. No staffers. No interns. Just President Wheeler sitting at his desk, repeatedly rubbing the stresses of the day from his forehead.

Emily and Deon steps closer to the desk. The President is unaware of their presence.

"Hey, Dad," Emily greets.

Reluctantly, the President raises his head.

"Honey, not now, please. It's just not a good time," the President pleads.

"Dad, Deon's leaving today. He wanted to say goodbye, that's all," Emily says.

President Wheeler sighs apologetically to Deon, "Sure, sure. Um, your father's from um, Kenya is it?"

"Actually, Nigeria, sir," Deon says respectfully.

It's plain to see that President Wheeler is surprised to hear the clear English from Deon's mouth, "Oh, you speak good English."

Instantly, Emily lowers her head in embarrassment at her father's naivety.

"Sir, English is our official language in Nigeria," Deon respectfully says.

Not a scholar by any means, once again, President Wheeler is genuinely surprised. Awkwardly, he doesn't know how to respond. Emily decides to save him by changing the subject.

"Dad, Deon wants to be a doctor," Emily injects.

"Wow, a doctor, huh?", the President nods to Deon.

Deon proudly answers, "Yes, sir. At first I was so afraid of coming to America to check out some of the prep schools and great medical universities here, but my father convinced me not to be afraid of something different because he said that we always learn things from something different."

Once again, President Wheeler is stunned by Deon's well-spoken maturity. The President sits awkwardly silent. And once more, Emily comes to her father's rescue.

"Well, Dad, we're gonna get out of your space now," Emily says.

"Sir, it's an honor to finally meet you, and good luck with the election in November," Deon respectfully nods.

"Thank you, Deon. I really needed to hear that today."

A few moments later, in the First Lady's office, while sipping on coffee, the First Lady and her assistant are pleasantly engaged with a TV campaign ad endorsing Senator April Taylor for President on the Sony widescreen mounted in the upper-left corner.

There's a knock at the door.

"Come in," the assistant answers.

Emily and Deon enter.

The First Lady looks at Emily and Deon then quietly points upward to the TV where the campaign ad for Senator Taylor is still running. As the TV ad slowly ends, the First Lady excitedly announces, "I know who's got my vote in November. She's got the stuff."

The assistant puts her coffee cup down then retrieves a nicely wrapped gift box from a nearby cabinet drawer.

The assistant places the colorful box atop the First Lady's desk.

"Go ahead, Deon, open it," the First Lady happily says.

Everyone stands around Deon as he peels away the fancy wrapping paper. Excitedly, Deon pulls out an expensive stethoscope from the box. Graciously, Deon steps closer to the First Lady then gives her a warm hug, "Thank you so much," he says.

"My pleasure, doctor," the First Lady says with great admiration in her voice.

Running the President's reelection campaign hasn't been easy for Nick and the White House staff, especially when the President's own wife blatantly does something completely contradictory to his own immigration policy. And the Lanterns' popularity across America has been a tremendous boost for Senator April Taylor as she continually gains more endorsements during her campaign. Although President Wheeler's approval rating has dwindled down greatly these past few months, he still has some true, die-hard supporters and some of them will be making their way to Richmond, Virginia later today for a gathering in Willy's backyard.

America: No Purchase Necessary

At the corner of Westmoreland Street and Cary Street Road, an eclectic group of scrappy kids on junk yard bikes have mustered together at Mary Munford Park, one of Richmond's well-maintained city parks. They seem to have gathered here for a reason, as if they're waiting for something and just killing time for now.

There's approximately twenty girls and boys of grade school age in this colorful group. They're mostly of ethnic backgrounds, some Mexican kids, Korean kids, African-American kids, East Indian kids, etc. There's an obvious difference in skin tone amongst this rainbow bunch, but what is equally apparent among this energetic group of kids is their love of bikes, and more specifically, their love and thrill of doing fancy bike tricks.

While gathered at one corner of the park, the young bikers are doing all kinds of BMX-style tricks on their bikes; one kid does a tail whip, several others are doing bunny hops, while a few are doing nose pivots.

No one in particular seems to be the leader, but one of the kids is getting a little antsy as he rides his bike towards the center of the group and complains, "He ain't coming. Who said that he was coming anyway?"

The other kids quickly chime in with their comments and thoughts...

"He is coming 'cause my daddy works with Willy at the car lot and he heard them talking about the President coming today."

"Whatcha mean car lot? That ain't no car lot. Willy sells them big ol' RV's over there. You don't even know whatcha be talking about so you need to be quiet."

"Even if he do come what y'all gonna do anyway?"

"We can take a picture with the President then flip it on Ebay."

"I don't wanna take a picture with him 'cause my mama say that he don't like people who got any kind of koolaid skin."

"Let's say we do get a picture and flip it on Ebay. How much you think we can get for it?"

"I don't know, maybe like a thousand."

"A thousand? Man, we can buy one of them good ramps with that kind of money!"

"Wait, how 'we gonna take a picture if we don't got a phone?"

A kid yanks out a cellphone from his back pocket then holds it up, "I gotta phone!," he excitedly says, and then he takes a closer look at the shattered screen on the phone.

Shamefully, the kid sighs, "I ain't gotta phone," then stuffs the broken phone back into his pants pocket.

"Why are riding around with a broken phone in yo' pocket?"

"Don't worry 'bout it. It's my phone. Ain't nobody else's."

⇌

Another kid from the back of the group raises her cellphone, "I gotta phone. It works."

"So, we ain't invited to that thing at Willy's so how 'we gonna get in then?"

"Easy. We're kids. Everybody likes kids. We're cute."

The scrappy kids begin to check each other out, looking at each other's weathered junk yard bikes, torn jeans, tattered shirts and beat-up sneakers as one of the girls nods reassuringly, "They'll let us in. We're just a bunch of cute kids."

Suddenly, three shiny black Cadillac Escalades cruise by the park, heading west on Cary Street Road.

One of the kids spots the President's motorcade passing by and excitedly alerts, "It's him! It's him! Look! It's the President! He's headed to Willy's!"

The kids turn their bikes westward then take off down Cary Street Road, pedaling as fast as they can behind the three Escalades.

Twenty minutes later, at 4970 Cary Street Road, the three glistening Escalades reach Will Benson's home. The President's motorcade slowly turns left onto the paved driveway leading to a luxurious mini-mansion with a perfectly-manicured front lawn ornamented with bountiful flower beds.

With bundles of campaign bumper stickers in their hands, two men are directing traffic onto the property and then motioning the President's motorcade to continue along the side yard towards the rear.

The vast backyard is sprawled with numerous SUV's and pickup trucks parked in no particular order along the right edge of the property.

Nearly all of the parked vehicles are plastered with Confederate Flags, Pro-Gun bumper stickers, and campaign bumper stickers proclaiming 'Wheeler For Wall' and 'Wheeler 4 More'.

Three men are double-checking the scaffolding of the makeshift stage along the left side of the spacious yard, as hordes of guests, casually dressed in airy summer skirts, blue jeans and t-shirts, are drinking beer and getting a bite to eat from the various BBQ grills bellowing smoke into the air.

Nearly twenty feet from the makeshift stage stands a thirty-foot high wooden cross stapled with enlarged photos of President Wheeler's opponent Senator April Taylor. At the base of the wooden cross is an ash pit encircled with large stones.

The three black Escalades find adequate parking further down the right edge of the property between a Dodge Ram and a Ford 250 pickup.

President Wheeler steps out of the second Escalade and is quickly surrounded by his Secret Service entourage. As the President and his security team walk up the yard, Will Benson, a burly man with an overly-friendly salesman smile, meets them halfway. He extends his hand to President Wheeler as the Secret Service agents keep a close eye.

"Hey, Mister President. Will Benson, but please, just Willy is fine."

Willy looks at the poker-face Secret Service agents and offers, "Y'all wanna beer or something?"

"They're on duty. They can't," President Wheeler interjects.

"Hell, that's the time to have a beer, when you're on duty. I betcha a little country juice will wipe that seriousness right off of them faces," Willy jokes.

Somewhat rudely, Willy throws his arm around President Wheeler then turns to face the watchful Secret Service agents and asks, "Hey, y'all ain't gonna shoot me if me and the President step over here for a little private chit chat, huh?"

President Wheeler nods to his security team that it's okay.

Willy leads the President a few feet away as the Secret Service agents eye them closely.

With an unpretentious, good ol' Southern boy charm, Willy says, "Mister President, I know that you don't know me and you gotta forgive me if I come on a little too strong but that's just who I am. I don't know if Jake told you or not but I take care of all of his Family Time RV dealerships while he looks over all of them burger joints. So, if you and your family ever need a fancy RV, kind of like that one them colored Lanterns or whatever the heck that family is who won that big sweepstakes. I tell ya', that was a real rip-off. That family should've never won that thing. They should've been disqualified with that Mexican kid with them, and plus, they gotta boy who dresses like girl. Ain't nothing American about that Lantern family, if you ask me. Anyway, you call me if you need anything 'cause I like you a lot and all of what you stand for, especially when you be talking about closing them borders. Me and all of my friends you see here today all think the same way you do and we're all glad you're here today."

Absorbing Willy's words while simultaneously gazing at the thirty-foot wooden cross stapled with the enlarged photos of Senator April Taylor's face, President Wheeler doesn't look very comfortable at all.

"So, Willy, what exactly is this cross?", the President asks.

"Glad you asked 'cause me and my buddies were all hoping that after you give your speech later on that maybe you'll be interested in sticking around for a few hours 'til the sun goes down and we're gonna light that bitch up and put a little fire in that woman's ass! Hell, if she became President I betcha this country ain't gonna feel like home anymore for people like you and me," Willy declares with strong conviction.

Abruptly, one of the men from the front yard begins to yell for Willy. The man loudly yells from the edge of the side yard, "Hey Willy! We gotta bunch of kids on bikes out front here who wanna see the President! Says they wanna take a picture with him!"

President Wheeler begins to smile at the thought of a group of children requesting to take a photo with him.

Along the side yard, the scrappy, colorful group of kids slowly ease their bikes beside the man yelling for Willy. Angrily, the man turns to the kids and barks, "I told you kids to stay in the front! Get back to the front!"

The kids stay put. No one moves a muscle.

Getting closer, Willy sees the kids. Willy's face tightens with disgust while eyeing the different skin tones amongst the kids. Furiously, Willy marches faster to the edge of the side yard to confront the defiant kids.

Willy growls at the kids, "This ain't the place for y'all. I don't want you kids here and the President don't want y'all here either, and he definitely ain't gonna take a picture with a wild looking bunch like y'all anyway."

Boldly, one of the kids steps closer to Willy and defiantly declares, "I betcha the President ain't said that. Probably just you said that."

"Look here you little bastard, who the hell you think you're talking to? Matter 'fact, I want all of y'all off my property right now! Get!", Willy barks.

Reluctantly, the kids turn their bikes around then ride away.

Standing a short distance away, President Wheeler heard every word exchanged between Willy and the kids. Quietly, the President gazes at Willy. A certain sadness begins to sip into the President's face as he realizes that the meanness and the hatred that he'd just witness in Willy is the same meanness and hatred that resides in him.

President Wheeler turns to his Secret Service team and sadly utters with a bit of defeat in his voice, "Let's get out of here, guys."

The President and the agents jump into the three Escalades to leave.

CHAPTER 12
SUNFLOWERS

It's two weeks later. The Lanterns are back home in Camden.

Earlier this morning, the youngest member of the family was picked up in a chauffeur-driven limo and taken an hour away to New York City where the extravagant Empire State Building and the new One World Trade Center highlight the renowned skyline.

Hordes of pedestrians and tourists fill the sidewalks of glitzy Time Square in Midtown Manhattan as taxis and limos pull up in front of the ritzy Sheraton along Seventh Avenue, dropping off well-dressed folks wearing pricey designer labels.

Today is a special day for young Ronnie as he gets treated as a VIP and a formal guest of one of America's most honored journalists.

In the spacious ballroom of the Sheraton Hotel a large banner runs above the stage. It reads, 'The Y. D'nar Foundation Journalism Awards'.

This prestigious, black tie affair has over three hundred attendees being tended to by a vigilant wait staff serving and replenishing their sumptuous meals and drinks.

Seated at one of the lavishly decorated tables in the center of the spacious room, a dapper eleven-year-old Ronnie, attired in a snazzy tuxedo, looks admiringly across the table at his date for the evening, New York World reporter Brittany Stills, who is elegantly adorned in a dashing gown.

A punctual MC is standing behind the podium on the stage. The MC looks to the left of the stage, nodding to a small group of assistants. One of the assistants retrieves a glistening gold-plated statuette from a wooden case conveniently placed nearby.

The MC steps closer to the mike, "And now ladies and gentlemen, the moment we've all been waiting for. For excellence in investigative reporting and journalism, the Y. D'nar Foundation proudly presents this year's Y. D'nar Award to Miss Brittany Stills of New York World."

The room erupts with applause.

On cue, the assistant brings the golden statuette on stage as Brittany stands and makes her way to the podium.

Brittany accepts the dazzling statuette then graciously nods 'thanks' to the MC and assistant as they turn to leave the stage.

The applause fades as Brittany steps closer to the microphone then, from her heart, calmly begins to speak, "We go through life gathering friends along the way. Some friends are manipulated and played with. Some friends are taken for granted. Some friends are bought, and most importantly though, some friends don't cost a dime."

Brittany pauses momentarily then makes eye contact with Ronnie seated at the center table.

Ronnie blushes as some of the guests at nearby tables begin to glance at him.

Brittany continues, "A few weeks ago I was watching TV and I saw a young man defending me in front of the President of the United States. That young man is my new friend, Ronnie Lantern, and I would like to dedicate this award to him."

The room burst into a round of applause as Brittany motions Ronnie to stand.

Humbly, Ronnie slowly stands as the gracious crowd explodes into another rousing applause.

Meanwhile, on Ferry Avenue in Camden, the Lanterns' once-weathered bungalow now looks bright and rejuvenated with its apparent new coat of paint. As a reminder of their long drive through rural Kansas, the once-drabby front yard is now being embellished with beautiful sunflower lawn ornaments as Darcy and Grandma Fannie stick a few of the colorful decorations into the ground, spaced about six feet apart.

Terri is helping out also as he, carefully and somewhat slowly, puts a fresh coat of white paint on the leaning, broken gate.

Rico exits the front door with a packed suitcase, and is followed by his father Eduardo, also carrying a stuffed suitcase.

Terri politely opens the gate as Rico takes the suitcase to a late-model Ford Ranger parked curbside. Eduardo stops in the middle of the yard. He turns toward Darcy and Grandma Fannie, gratefully nods, "Fannie and Darcy, I can't thank you enough for taking in my son. If you need anything at all, please come see us. We're only six blocks away."

"Aw, Mister Garcia, you and Rico is family," Darcy quickly responds.

Suddenly, the front door swings open! All heads turn towards the door. With an apparent throw pillow snugly tucked underneath her t-shirt, Latoya appears at the doorway and loudly announces, "Mama, you ain't gonna believe this but after Rico done knocked me up and finds out that the ultrasound says that there's three babies in here 'he just gonna up and leave me! Now what kind of man is that?"

Amused, Rico, Eduardo and Terri crack smiles and chuckle at Latoya's antics.

"Latoya, sweetheart, I'm gonna keep you in my prayers," Grandma Fannie teases.

Darcy turns to Rico and quips, "Hey Rico, betcha wish them six blocks was more like six miles now, huh?"

Latoya shoots her mother a dirty look then yanks the pillow from under her t-shirt then throws it at Darcy, "Oh, shut up, Mama."

"More like sixty miles," Rico jokes.

Latoya freezes then shoots Rico a look with a teasing, "Shut up, Rico."

Eduardo and his son load the suitcases unto the back of the Ford Ranger then hops into their seats.

⇌

Before Rico has a chance to buckle his seatbelt, seemingly out of nowhere, there's Latoya standing outside the passenger side window, silently yearning for a hug.

Without hesitation, Rico happily steps out of the pickup to give Latoya a long, warm embrace.

A sparkling 2020 Lexus RX is slowly cruising down Ferry Avenue then comes to a stop directly across the street from the Lanterns' home.

As Eduardo and Rico takes off in their Ranger, a gorgeous lady, the embodiment of brains and beauty, steps out of the shiny Lexus with an air of confidence and walks directly toward Terri next to the leaning gate.

A business card dangles from her fingers as she approaches Terri, "Hm, I like that. A painter with a legal mind. Are you Terri?"

Standing with the paint brush in his right hand, Terri scans his brain momentarily, trying to figure out why does this lady know his name and who in the world is she, and then it hits him, "Oh, that's right. You must be Sherry's friend."

Politely, Terri gestures that he can't shake hands due to the paint brush and bits of white paint sprinkled on his hands. Pleasantly, the lady nods 'that's okay' as she introduces herself, "I'm Rayna Fullerton. Me and Sherry were pretty tight during those school years."

"Hm, tight? How tight?", Terri asks with a curious grin.

"Oh, she didn't tell you, huh? That's just like her. You see, Sherry loves the corporate world so she sort of plays their game, you know, like keeping your real true self hidden just to keep the six-figure salary, but I, on the other hand, will eat your ass alive in court", Rayna gives Terri a knowing wink, letting him know that she is fully aware of the traumatic incident which sparked his interest in wanting to become a lawyer, and then she continues, "I will eat their ass in any courtroom if anyone ever try to kick a group of innocent teenagers out of an ice cream parlor simply because the manager didn't like their gender identity or sexual orientation."

Coolly, Rayna hands her business card to Terri. He accepts it in his left hand as Rayna continues to appeal to his legal interest, "Terri, I'm sorry about what happened to you and your friends at that ice cream shop. We have an office in Cherry Hill. We'll start you in as a paid intern, you can get certified as a paralegal, and if you stick with us, I'll set you up for law school. And, by the way, I know about your prize money. Keep it. I got lots of friends. We'll get you into law school. Don't worry about finances for now, passing the bar is enough to worry about."

⇒╀╀⇐

Terri is blown away with emotions. He stands completely dumbfounded, then utters, "Wow, Sherry did this?"

Rayna quickly nods, "Actually, you did this. I've known Sherry for a long time, and she's not the type to pull strings just for any ol' body. She had to have seen something special about you Terri. Trust me. This is all you. And I hope you'll be at the office bright and early Monday morning. When you get there just tell them I sent you."

Rayna gives Terri a 'goodbye' wink then coolly walks back across the street to her car. Still overwhelmed with emotion, Terri stares at Rayna's business card in one hand as white paint slowly drips from the paint brush in the other hand.

Latoya looks at Terri briefly then shift her eyes to the half-painted gate he's been working on since earlier today. Latoya's not going to pass up an opportunity to take a crack at her brother, "Hey Terri, can I ask you a question? About how long would you say it takes the average person to paint a gate?"

Holding their stomach, Darcy and Grandma Fannie double over with laughter as Latoya takes another playful stab at her brother, "Mama, I swear, he's been painting that gate ever since this morning."

Terri shoots Latoya a look then teases, "Girl, you be quiet. At least I'm out here doing something. What 'you doing?"

Quick-witted Latoya fires back, "I did as much as you did on that gate, which is nothing!"

Darcy and Grandma Fannie can't control their laughter as they nearly tumble to the ground.

Seconds later, something bright and glaring further down the street catches Latoya's eye, "Oh, Mama, look at that! It's Dad!"

Latoya excitedly points down Ferry Avenue at the gleaming bus turning the corner and headed towards the Lanterns' home.

The luxury, flag-colored RV that took the Lanterns across the country and back has been repainted gold and purple, and converted into an upscale tour bus with vibrant side panels proudly boasting 'REGGIE'S REGAL TOURS'.

It's November. Election night. It's late and all of the numbers are in. At a hotel ballroom in Washington, with TV and photographers' cameras aimed at him, President Wheeler is making his concession speech before a somber crowd.

The First Lady, standing next to her husband on the right, is trying her best to conceal a triumphant smile as their daughter Emily stands closely to her father's left.

The President turns to Emily with an apologetic glance as her profound forearm tattoo of Japanese characters momentarily steals his attention then continues his speech, "America has spoken, and right now I would like to congratulate President-elect April Taylor on becoming the first woman President of the United States of America. And, as for me, well, let me just say this," awkwardly the President begins to speaks in Japanese, "Nana korobi ya oki", and then he oddly switches back to English, "I might fall down, but Dennis Wheeler always get back up."

Meanwhile, at their new apartment in Camden, Eduardo and his son Rico are watching the President's concession speech in the living room. Eduardo shakes his head in disgust while listening to President Wheeler misuse and butcher such an honorary Japanese proverb.

"Man, that dude's still at it. Is he ever gonna learn?", Rico sighs.

"Don't worry, Rico. God's gonna make him pay for turning something good into something ugly. He already lost his job, so I don't know what else is gonna happen to him," Eduardo groans.

CHAPTER 13
TOMORROW

Ever since Grandma Fannie's been back Red's been planning to have her over to his place for a special dinner, just the two of them. Tonight's the night.

Red's been living by himself for so long that when he'd set his kitchen table for this very special date, it didn't readily occur to him that his paper plates maybe slightly out of place for this particular occasion.

So far, things are going great. Fannie was excited about this dinner date with Red also, so much so that she even put on some lipstick that she'd borrowed from Latoya.

"How's the meatloaf, Fannie?"

"Not bad, Red. I'm impressed. A lot of folks leave it in the oven too long and it comes out so dry, but this ain't dry at all."

"Thank you, Fannie. Meatloaf is the only thing I can make on my own. Everything else I kind of get out of a box."

Red looks at Fannie with a certain flicker in his eye. Fannie catches his gaze. They know that something special is in the air tonight but both are a little apprehensive to make the first move.

Along with his meatloaf made from scratch, Red has glasses of red wine placed next to their paper plates. Fannie softly smiles at Red's paper plates but doesn't say anything out of kindness.

Fannie takes a sip of her wine, then slowly eases into something more personal, "By the way, I want to thank you again for stopping those Devil boys from breaking in our house when we were gone."

"Oh, that was nothing. Just like I'd told them boys, you are the sweetest lady in this neighborhood. They had no business trying to do something like that to somebody as sweet as you, Fannie."

Fannie blushes, "Oh, Red, stop."

Red reaches down and retrieves a shiny gift bag with a beautiful bow and a card attached. Red reaches across the table and hands the shiny bag to Fannie.

"I got you a little something, Fannie."

"Oh, what a pretty bag. You didn't have to do that, Red."

Fannie opens the bag and carefully dig out the Afrocentric necklace and Afrocentric card. Amused, Fannie smiles and politely says, "Now, Red, you're trying too hard."

"I really like you, Fannie. You know, when you gave me that CD with that old country song on it I started thinking about those awful things I'd said to my daughter and her friend years ago. I wish that I could somehow take it all back. That song really brought up some old memories of back home. I don't wanna be that same guy anymore, Fannie."

As Red fight back tears, Fannie slowly rises from her chair then gives him a much-needed hug. The somewhat casual hug soon turns into a tender embrace as Fannie's lipstick begins to smear on Red's cheeks.

⇌⇋

"I always knew that my grandma and Mister Coles would get together 'cause they always looked at each other like they belonged together," Ronnie concludes.

As Ronnie finishes his story and begins to rise from the cushion chair besides the teacher's desk, Miss Pritchett asks the rest of the class, "Are there any questions for Ronnie?"

Big Riley, Troy, and most of the sixth graders in Ronnie's class sit quietly, all except for Monica Mennison, who looks at Ronnie with a cynical sneer then says, "Ronnie, in your story you talked about America having our first woman President now, like it's a real good thing. Do you actually think she'll be any different than the men before her? They don't care about us kids, none of them do."

Sounding mature beyond his years, calmly Ronnie responds, "I don't know about all of that but my story was just about my family and hopefully it had some hope in, you know, kind of like hoping that things get better not just here in Jersey but better all over America. We need a better tomorrow."

EPILOGUE

A couple weeks after our last 'Sit and Talk' in Miss Pritchett's class, Monica got expelled from school. Monica can't come back to Camden Middle 'cause she wrote some letters to the Camden School District telling them that if they don't install solar panels in all of the public schools in Camden then somebody will pay a big price. And when Monica's mom tried to tell the superintendent that what her daughter probably had meant to say was that the school district's electric bill would be higher if they didn't switch to solar panels. But Monica was at that same meeting, standing right next to her mom, and Monica corrected her mom right in front of the superintendent and said 'No, Mom, I meant what I said, somebody will pay a big price, just like the letters said.'"

Camden Middle won't be the same anymore. Miss Pritchett is moving to Silver Lake, California in a few months. I told her that I'm going to miss her 'Sit and Talk' days, and that if I become a teacher one day, I'm gonna have a 'Sit and Talk' day every month too.

And, I guess ain't nothing keeping Mister Coles and my grandma apart anymore. Last night, Grandma spent the whole night at Mister Coles' house, and I think they're gonna be living together now.

Other Books By Author Randolph Randy Camp

1. 'Wet Matches: A Novel'
2. '...Then The Rain'
3. 'False Dandelions'
4. '29 Dimes: A Love Story'

Copyright Information

1. U.S. Copyright Office Registration Number: PAu004078468
   (Sole) Author: Randolph Randy Camp
   U.S. Copyright Registration Date: June 4, 2020
   *(June Fourth, Twenty-Twenty)
2. Writers Guild of America, West Registration Number: 2062389
   (Sole) Author: Randolph Randy Camp
   WGA, West Registration Date: June 12, 2020
   *(June Twelfth, Twenty-Twenty)

ABOUT THE AUTHOR

Born on March 12, 1961 in rural Spotsylvania County, Virginia, Randolph Randy Camp witnessed racial and economic inequality during his childhood. Creating colorful characters and writing stories have always been a welcomed escape and a much-needed distraction during Randy's sometimes bleaker periods.

After graduating from Spotsylvania High School in 1979, Randy enlisted into the U.S. Air Force and traveled the globe.

At the heart of most of Randy's stories is the central theme of triumph-over-tragedy, as a way of offering hope and sympathy to his readers. Randy won the Quarter-Finals Prize at The Writers Network 14th Annual Screenplay and Fiction Competition for his story 'Wet Matches'. After the national and international attention from the publication of 'Wet Matches: A Novel', Randy was honored from The White House with the President's Volunteer Service Award on January 15, 2012 for bringing more awareness to the social issues of teen runaways and youth homelessness throughout America.

Aside from his love of writing, Randy also has a passion for working with at-risk and troubled youth. In 2015, Randy graduated and received an Associate of Science Degree in Mental Health Counseling from Erie Community College in New York.

Currently, Randy resides in Des Moines, Iowa. Randy has five daughters Natasha, Melinda, Randie, Ranielle, Christina and one son Joshua. Two of Randy's favorite quotes are 'Don't let others define you – You define yourself!' and 'Be yourself, don't be afraid to dream Big!'

CPSIA information can be obtained
at www.ICGtesting.com
Printed in the USA
LVHW080730240821
695886LV00007B/725